JULIAN FANE

The author was born in 1927 and spent his childhood at Lyegrove near Badminton in Gloucestershire. The garden there was created by his mother and noted for its beauty. He is married and now lives in Sussex.

'A unique contribution to the literature of childhood . . . curiously intuitive . . . the brilliant thing about Mr Fane's method is that he always chooses the small, believable incident and manages to x-ray its significance as part of a spiritual adventure – the adventure upon which every hero of literature has been engaged'

The Saturday Review

'Quite exceptionally good. It is a novel I feel I shall never forget . . . faultless – for a man so young, a triumph'

Encounter

'A work of clear beauty. A rare and radiant grace pervades its pages. A remarkably integrated whole work, profoundly moving, in which the intensive exploration of the world of a small boy turns into a captivating illumination of human nature and its common joys and burdens. It is prose fiction of rare, memorable, almost incomparable beauty'

New York Times Book Review

'Sensitively named, it is indeed the story of a 'morning', of a fragment in the long day of a lifetime, and like the morning, it has the washed air, the shimmer, and the vulnerability with which certain new days begin. Accurately and poignantly, Mr Fane catches the moment, in the garden of the soul, between bud and flower. Here in MORNING is the tiny individual miracle, which, forever and everywhere multiplied, reveals all the seminality of life itself'

New York Herald Tribune

'Combines an extraordinary, strong, fresh sense of reality with an unfailing sense of art . . . MORNING is the most distinguished first novel I have read for several years'

Lord David Cecil

'A beautiful story . . . Neither hackneyed nor sentimental'

The Illustrated London News

'In one aspect this book is a useful Parents' Companion. It may convince young fathers that they should be less obtuse and shy'

Harold Nicolson in the Observer

Julian Fane

MORNING

First published in Great Britain in 1956 by John Murray (Publishers) Ltd.

Hamish Hamilton Ltd, and St George's Press Ltd edition, 1986
Sceptre edition 1988

Sceptre is an imprint of Hodder and Stoughton Paperbacks, a division of Hodder and Stoughton Ltd.

British Library C.I.P.

Fane, Julian
Morning
I. Title
823'.914[F]   PR6056.A57

ISBN 0-340-41920-2

The characters and situations in this book are entirely imaginary and bear no relation to any real person or actual happening

Printed and bound in Great Britain for Hodder and Stoughton Paperbacks, a division of Hodder and Stoughton Ltd., Mill Road, Dunton Green, Sevenoaks, Kent TN13 2YA (Editorial Office: 47 Bedford Square, London, WC1 3DP) by Richard Clay Ltd., Bungay, Suffolk. Photoset by Rowland Phototypesetting Ltd., Bury St Edmunds, Suffolk.

CONTENTS

For J. C. F.

1938

ONE

A DAY

A figure appears in the open schoolroom french windows at the corner of the house, raises her hand against the brightness and calls, 'Vere?'

The seven-year-old boy on the terrace, staggering under the weight of three half-rotten planks, answers, 'I'm coming!' Then, conscious of being concealed from view, he carries the planks to the wall that borders the grove of trees and carefully drops them over. One breaks. He turns away, considering the uses of the broken plank, picks up his tweed coat, feels in the pockets for the box of matches and the five cigarettes in their fragile paper holder, folds the coat across his arm and walks on down the terrace.

Suddenly he begins to run, leaping and skipping, revelling in the sunshine, in the summer, in his schemes and ambitions, in the reliability of his leather shorts and the springiness of the rubber soles of his sandals.

'I'm coming, Mal,' he calls. 'I'm coming.'

Mal is now standing on the smooth grass of the lawn, looking as if she had been planted there many years before like some proud and ancient tree. At the sight of the boy she exclaims in her singsong voice, savouring the Frenchness of her accent and the sweet airs of the day, 'Oh, darling, it's so lovely, isn't it? Do you see the blue sky? I love it so!' And she gestures comprehensively with her hand, flirting it somehow in a gay lighthearted fashion.

'Quelle vie,' says Vere, teasing.

'Quelle vie, quelle vie! I love it so!' Enjoying the joke she starts regretfully for the schoolroom door. Her walk is heavy, powerful. 'Now lessons, darling. Les leçons, les leçons,' she chants.

They sit together at the schoolroom table, enveloped in a cloud of the scent Mal always uses, half eau-de-Cologne, half disinfectant. Furniture looms into view as their eyes grow accustomed to the shade. Scamp the dog sleeps in the sunlight on the paving outside.

'And then, you see,' Vere is saying, trying to convey something of his excitement, 'my house is going to have two rooms. At least two rooms. And it'll be watertight, so that I can sleep in it. And have a fire . . .' He notices a flicker of amusement on the lips and in the brown eyes, and continues in a changed persuasive tone. 'Besides, it's going to be so useful. Probably I shall live there most of the time . . .' He breaks off, knowing that he has overstated his case.

Mal laughs, losing the high poise of her head. 'But chéri mignon,' she says, 'with what are you building your house?'

'Oh – odds and ends and bits and pieces.'

He is content to joke. He is prepared to wait for his moment of triumph. When the house is finished that will come. He imagines the admiring throng, the cries of wonder and congratulation, the stream of eager visitors. He laughs partly because he knows that one day his house will be no laughing matter.

The room is cool. He begins to put on his coat, cautiously, remembering its delicate precious cargo.

'And now,' Mal says, 'we must work. We will turn out your pockets, come along.'

Oh glory, thinks Vere. Pleasure, sunshine, dreams are swept away. The room is black and stifling. Why did he put on his coat? He does not even need it.

Mal points to his breast pocket. 'Et maintenant, qu 'est-ce que c 'est?'

'The handkerchief.'

'Le mouchoir.'

'Le mouchoir,' he repeats, thinking, Fool, fool. He has

missed his chance, already it is too late to avoid the inquisition. He should have rebelled at once. Or does she know his secret? Did she search his pockets when his coat lay on the terrace wall?

'Allons vite, mon chéri, vite!'

The situation is beyond his control. He is hot, unhappy. He delves into the pockets of his leather shorts, pulls out string, chewing-gum, his knife. He repeats the names of the objects automatically as they are placed on the table before him. His hand rattles the box of matches: he raises his voice to drown the sound. He understands nothing, all is altered. Mal is unsparing: he is lost.

'Le couteau, la ficelle . . .'

He cannot bring himself to say, 'Why, Mal, that's everything.' He imagines too clearly the plunging hand, the withdrawal of the green paper holder, the merciless question: 'Et ces cigarettes, Vere?' Even if Mal does not know – and obviously she does, she is playing with him cruelly – but whether she does or not, disaster is still bound to overtake him: the cigarettes will fall from his pocket, the matches spontaneously ignite. He wonders if he should kill Mal, run away, make a last stand in his house. He is really a fugitive, a desperate man.

And his pockets are nearly empty. His fingers close over the box of matches, release them for the tenth time, pry into the deepest recesses, touch something and emerge.

'A feather, Mal!'

'Une plume.'

'Une plume.'

And now, now there is no turning back. He slaps the pockets of his coat, in the manner of his father, absent-mindedly almost. The matches rattle.

'Why, that's funny,' he says, opening his pocket wide with both hands and peering in. 'I seem to have a box of matches, don't I?' He looks Mal full in the face. A heady freedom possesses him. He begins to laugh. 'I wonder how they got there, don't you, Mal? A box of matches, dear, dear.'

He lays the matches on the table, a little away from the

other trophies, and for a second both he and Mal regard them with surprise and interest.

'Les allumettes, Vere.'

'Les allumettes.'

'Les all-um-ettes . . .' There is a finality in her tone, a twinkle in the brown eyes. 'Et maintenant, la dictée.'

Vere begins to refill his pockets, the mirth still welling inside him. Mal, with a precise movement, stretches the waxed cover of the exercise book and writes in her strong script: 'Dictée. Le 2 Mai, 1938.' The matches remain on the table.

'I'd better leave those matches here, hadn't I, Mal?' he inquires. 'They might come in useful, for lighting fires or something.'

'Merci, Vere.'

Suddenly such a feeling of love seizes the boy, such a warmth of affection, such gratitude, such relief and such joy overflow in him that he is sure – he is certain – his heart must break. He catches hold of the large hand, kisses the cheek and lays his head on the soft shoulder, talking and laughing. He has never been so happy, never known the world could be so full and kind, so true and beautiful. He makes Mal gobble like a turkey and produce the potato she keeps in the top of her stocking against the rheumatism: he whistles through the gap in his teeth and blows through his fingers, imitating the hoot of an owl: he invites Mal to be the first to visit his house: and little by little the storm of emotion subsides. The dictation book is opened, the exercise book is arranged at the correct angle, the paper begins to wrinkle under the heat of the small hand, the voice to intone and the uncertain characters to spread across the page.

'Où est le chat de ma tante . . . ?'

Scamp the dog, drunk with the sun, struggles to her feet, waddles indoors and collapses with a sigh. The razor-edged shaft of light swings imperceptibly from right to left over the pale carpet. Sounds break from time to time, electric with distracting associations, into the somnolent peace of the schoolroom.

Bella the parlourmaid is starting to lay for luncheon. Her

prim step clips across the oak floor of the dining-hall next door, stopping mysteriously when they reach the rug. Silver clinks at intervals as it is placed on the long refectory table, and the hand-bell tinkles, muted, discreet. Out of doors the iron rim of a wheelbarrow crunches lethargically over the grey gravel of the drive. Bruise and Harris, the undergardeners, are weeding and smoothing the square turnabout in front of the house. From farther away comes the quick clatter of horse's hooves; somebody shouts. Vere imagines his father, thumbs hooked in the pockets of his coat, one foot turned outwards, lips pursed as he softly whistles, eyeing a nervous animal. Voices are heard; a car; the sweep of twig brushes; cries of fledgling birds; bees.

The clock on the mantelpiece whirrs and chimes.

'Mal, can I go now?'

'Yes, darling, yes. C'est fini!'

Vere runs through the french windows, sees his father advancing from the other end of the house, breaks into an imitative walk as he goes to meet him, bending his legs loosely at the knees and thrusting a hand in his trouser pocket, and calls out a greeting.

His father says, 'What have you been doing, you little monkey?' and pretends to squeeze the boy's nose between the fingers of his clenched fist. 'Have you been good?'

Vere laughs and says, 'You've been looking at a horse, haven't you?'

'How do you know that?'

'I heard you. I guessed.'

'What a clever boy you are.' The blue eyes crinkle at the corners in the way that Vere loves and the humorous quacking noise is made with the side of the mouth.

'Dad, are you staying here this afternoon?'

'No, old boy, I'm playing golf. I must change.'

'Will you drive an old golf ball into the wood?'

'I will tomorrow. You go and see what Nanny's doing.' A double quacking noise: the long legs mount the stairs two at a time, unevenly: the hard wood screeches beneath the clusters of nails in the shoes: a door slams.

Vere swings on the banisters. 'Bella,' he says, 'can you whistle through your teeth?'

'No, Master Vere,' she replies shortly, folding the napkins.

He wonders if she has something wrong with her teeth. But surely not, he decides; they look so incredibly white and even. 'My front tooth's loose,' he says. She does not answer. 'Bella, what's the time?

'Ten to one, Master Vere.'

Ten minutes to luncheon: nothing to do: no time for anything. A delivery-van is bumping along the back-drive. He runs out of the house and over the paving and gazes through the gate in the garden wall. The van sways round the dovecote and pulls up in a perfect position, hidden by a circular yew-tree from the nursery windows. It is Mr Trent the baker from Long Cretton.

Vere lifts the latch of the gate and saunters towards the van. 'Oh, good morning, Mr Trent,' he says. 'How are you?'

'Why, Master Vere, good morning. I'm nicely, thanks, and how's yourself? Come to see what I've brought along, have you? Let's take a look.'

'I was on my way in actually,' Vere protests, following the baker to the rear of the van.

The doors are unlocked and opened. The sweet smell of fresh-baked bread assails his nostrils. Mr Trent, talking all the while, searches under the crisp loaves for the white cardboard box. He finds it, shakes it, clasps his hands together. 'What have we here?' He laughs. The box is crammed with bars of chocolate.

'They do look delicious,' Vere enunciates with difficulty, his mouth watering, his fingers twisting the sixpence in his pocket.

'They are delicious too! Now what are we going to have today? These Mars bars are very nice, and so are the Crunchies, and here are some whipped-cream walnuts. Oh, just you look at them – but don't tell Nurse, Master Vere!'

'How much are the Milky Ways, Mr Trent?' Vere asks hurriedly.

'The Milky Ways are very very good. They're tuppence.'

'Can I have a Milky Way then, please? No, perhaps I'll have two, please.'

'Two Milky Ways. Not three? That'll be fourpence, Master Vere, and mum's the word.'

Vere pays his sixpence and receives his change. But then he hesitates.

The baker says, 'What, Master Vere, I do declare, you haven't seen your favourites today,' and the fatal tray full of cream-buns is held out for inspection.

The buns are brown and soft and slit in the middle, and the scent of the cream with the indescribable flavour which rests in the slits is wafted upwards.

'I can't afford one,' Vere says faintly.

Mr Trent seems not to hear him. In a voice as creamy and tantalising as his buns he continues, 'Isn't that a pretty sight? Shall I tell you what we'll do? You keep your tuppence. Now you choose a little favourite. How's that? – But eat it up quick, before Nurse catches you. Oh listen, there's the bell!'

Vere feels liquid with desire and apprehension. The luncheon bell is ringing from the nursery window, the forbidden bun is proffered temptingly, the pennies are already in his pocket, time is passing. If only Mr Trent had come earlier. The lack of appetite at luncheon will be suspect for certain.

'Thank you very much, Mr Trent. Good morning.'

Vere takes the bun. His hand is trembling though his voice is controlled. He walks with faltering steps towards the stable archway, sits on the stone mounting-block, bolts the bun in four mouthfuls, unable to indulge the ecstasy of the cream-filling, runs into the yard and across it, and starts to climb the fire-escape to the nursery window.

Mr Trent calls up to him, 'See you tomorrow, Master Vere!' and puts his finger to his lips as he enters the house.

Vere hiccups, squeezes through the window, drops onto the floor, then goes into the day-nursery. Flora the nursery-maid is trying to decide if she has laid correctly for luncheon. Her eyes when she looks at him are wide and abstracted.

'Flora, I've got you a present,' he says, giving her a Milky Way.

'Oh Vere, you shouldn't have.' Her voice is caressing, rather broken, sometimes throaty, sometimes clear. 'You haven't been with Mr Trent?'

'Don't tell Nanny, Flora.'

She jerks her head in a manner denoting trouble in store, the eyebrows raised and the tongue clicking, and sends him to wash his hands.

When he returns luncheon is on the table. There is a dish with a domed silver cover: two vegetable dishes stand beside it. He hopes they contain something fresh and tasty: roast beef, for instance, dark sharp gravy, flowery boiled potatoes and those French beans, succulent and steaming, scraped to a tender green and with the strings removed. – That is what he could eat today, that is what he would prefer above everything. Nanny enters, the baby is strapped into the high chair, grace is said. Vere closes his eyes, praying fervently for French beans. The lids are lifted.

Under the silver dome is a fricassée of chicken, drops of melted butter gilding its rich surface. Mashed potato and stalky spring greens have been squashed flat by the covers of the other dishes.

'Not too much for me, please, Nanny,' Vere says, and to hide his despair turns to the baby. 'Hullo, Faith. Hullo, Faithie.'

The baby, gazing greedily at the food and kicking her chair, seizes his finger in a vice-like grip.

'Where's your appetite, Vere?' Nanny asks.

'Let go of my finger, Faith. I'm just not hungry, I'm afraid.'

'You'll never grow up to be big and strong if you don't eat.'

I will, he thinks with dull rcsentment. A plate is laid before him and he starts to pick half-heartedly at the white concoction. Everything tastes of Mr Trent's bun.

Nanny says, 'Now Vere, eat up this minute.'

The rebuke injures him. He assumes a reproachful expression, but a chasm of sharp indigestion suddenly yawns beneath him. Faith's excited cries between each mouthful, the click of cutlery, the twittering flutter of the budgerigars – all are unpleasant, threatening. He cannot move – he must not even try: the weight of his fork disturbs his balance: the sunlight is too bright and too hot: he feels sick.

'Come along, sweetheart, eat a bit for me.'

'No, thank you, Flora.'

The care with which he speaks makes the words sound cold. He attempts to smile at Flora, but manages only a pained grimace.

'And it's no good making up to Flora,' Nanny says. 'Just get on with your lunch.'

He denies the accusation. But now his voice, instead of ringing tart and rebellious as intended, sounds sour and sulky, and he immediately wishes he had kept silent.

'And please don't answer back, Vere,' Nanny adds.

The baby, stimulated by the currents of discord in the atmosphere, grins round the table and turns a vacant windy stare on her brother.

'Oh Faith, go away,' he says.

The baby cries.

'That's wasn't kind, Vere, I'm surprised at you,' Nanny says as she comforts the child. 'Poor Faith. You ought to be more gentle with your little sister. There there now, there.'

What has happened, what has he done? He ate a cream-bun: it is his own affair. There is no need for anyone to be upset or cross. He tries to show by a gesture that he wishes Faith at any rate no harm, but her face grows purple as his hand approaches and her bellows drive the budgerigars half mad.

'Now Vere!' Nanny exclaims. 'You're being most aggravating. Leave the poor girl alone for any sake.'

Faith is unstrapped, swung soothingly in Nanny's arms until her bellows become sobs and then gurgles, replaced in her chair and coaxed into accepting another spoonful of food.

Vere meanwhile sits silent and hunched at the table, his hands in his lap, his eyes on a mustard-pot. He no longer feels sick, only miserable. He studies the mustard-pot. He is expected to cry, he knows it, but he will not, he will not – nothing will make him.

'Please, sweetheart, please, you must eat up, you know.'

He does not answer. He cannot. Flora's soft voice, the

whole idea of Flora and her kindness and love, is insupportable, the blow for which he is not prepared. His eyes prick and he is unable to control the quivering of his lower lip. The outline of the mustard-pot blurs, the lump in his throat prevents him from swallowing. A tear trickles down his cheek, quick and damp, and falls onto his leather shorts.

'Do you want my handkerchief, sweetheart?'

'No.'

His heart is hardening. He glares at the mustard-pot. Indignation mingles with his brimming self-pity. He can never be the same: gone is the tender amenable boy who sat down at the table. As Nanny will learn, he in his turn can be harsh and cruel and unforgiving. Such, henceforth, is going to be his natural state, and no apologies or pleas will ever recall that other Vere.

Nanny asks Flora, 'Have you any idea why he can't eat?'

Flora pauses. 'He's never much appetite, has he?'

'But he must eat something. A growing boy.'

'Shall I make you a castle, Vere, and you can eat it up?'

'All right, Flora,' he agrees, forgetting his notions of revenge and suddenly feeling hungry.

'You've not been eating sweets, Vere?'

'No,' he replies in a shocked voice, taking an active interest in the lay-out of the castle, the moat of sauce, the walls of mashed potato and the wood of greens in the castle grounds. 'What about a drawbridge? Oughtn't it to have a drawbridge?' He makes the query general, but Nanny supplies no answer. She is not to be diverted. He feared as much. He might as well try to divert the sea. He looks at Flora hopelessly. 'It ought to have a drawbridge,' he says.

'Has Mr Trent been up today?' Nanny asks.

'Mr Trent? I think he has,' says Vere.

'I see.'

'Shall I eat some of the moat, Flora?'

'What did Mr Trent give you, Vere?'

'Thank you, Flora – look, the moat is leaking now!'

'Those buns, I suppose, Vere?'

'Wait a minute, Nanny!'

'Has Vere been eating buns, Flora?'

'Oh, oh, the moat is running away –'

'Please answer me, Flora. Has Vere been eating Mr Trent's buns?'

'Yes,' he interrupts, 'I have been eating buns.'

Everyone is surprised, even the baby. Nanny is the first to collect herself.

'Well Vere, in that case you're a very naughty boy,' she says.

'I only ate one,' he replies. 'And I don't feel hungry. And that's all.' He looks boldly about him. He is really strong and daring enough for anything.

'That's most disobedient of you, Vere. And Mr Trent ought to be ashamed of himself.'

'But I made Mr Trent give me the bun.'

'What?'

'I made him, I forced him.'

The baby laughs. Vere joins in and pats her head. The baby goes on laughing, then begins to grind her five teeth.

'Don't do that, Faith. Vere, listen to me please. Vere!' Nanny and Flora exchange a bewildered glance. 'You are a bad boy. If you eat Mr Trent's buns again I shall punish you. And this is my last warning. Now finish what you can of your lunch and hurry up about it.'

'Yes, Nanny,' he says, and a minute later adds with a penitent smile, 'I'm sorry.'

After luncheon Flora disappears with Faith. Vere fetches his book, takes it to Nanny and begs her to read aloud to him. She puts down her newspaper, and while he curls himself up at the other end of the sofa, looks for their place and then in a steady voice begins.

The story is about Little Jack Rabbit and his mother, and their home under the Bramble Patch in Sunny Meadow. The characters are varied, kind Owl and wily Danny Fox, the scene golden and evocative. Vere listens rapt, translating the wonderful tale into terms of his own experience, placing the Bramble Patch and Shady Forest, until Nanny's head gradually sinks forward. He watches her jerk it upright, but only half-listens when she resumes her reading. The square glass clock ticks away on the mantelpiece, the heavy pendulum swings. Again the words slur and drag. Nanny jerks her head a second time.

'Vere, I'm sorry,' she says, 'but I can't read another word. We'll have some more tomorrow. Go to sleep for a minute. And I'll have forty winks, my eyes are just closing.'

She shuts the book and puts it to one side, folds her arms and allows her head to droop. Even in repose her compact figure is alert and energetic. Vere listens for her light reassuring breathing. Soon he is sleeping too.

When he awakes the nursery is empty. He jumps off the sofa, runs along the nursery passage and down the stairs, steals two ginger biscuits from the tin in the pantry, pockets a box of matches and goes out to his house. For a while he regards it critically, munching the biscuits and considering what he must do. Then he sets to work.

The shadows have deepened under the chestnut trees. Wood pigeons coo in the high branches and make leisurely flights, dipping, rising, clapping their wings behind their backs. A distant cuckoo calls and a horse whinnies and stamps its feet in the stable-yard. The earth seems to drowse in the afternoon sunlight, peaceful, replete.

For an hour and a half Vere works without pause. Then, his head aching slightly from his exertions and his hands shaking, he sits on the trunk of a fallen tree and produces the packet of cigarettes from his pocket. He selects a cigarette and puts it in the corner of his mouth. Deliberately, as if his mind were on other things, he opens the new box of matches, strikes a match and shields the flame professionally against a non-existent breeze. He puffs, shakes out the match, flicks it away and looks at the cigarette to see that it is fairly lit.

This is the well-earned rest from his labours, the reward. He surveys his work, finding some cause for satisfaction. He has made progress, there is no doubt about it, but tomorrow he will redouble his efforts. He must have some long nails and the head of that hammer needs attention. What a lot there is to be done, more even than he thought.

Blue-grey smoke from his cigarette spirals and drifts languidly in the air. Its redolence suggests maturity and honest toil and skilled workmanship. He clenches and unclenches his hand, enjoying the thought that his palms are hardening and his muscles growing strong, and puffs again at his cigarette. Smoke gets into his eyes. The sudden sharp pain makes him rise to his feet, but a dizziness overcomes him, his head swims, and he quickly sits down again and blindly stubs out the cigarette. He doubles himself up and rests his head on his knees, keeping his eyes tightly closed. The dizziness passes and also the pain in his eyes, and the mood of quiet confidence and pride returns. Two or three days at this rate should make a big difference . . . He stands up, swings his coat over his shoulder and starts to plod towards the house, a real labourer, hungry, thirsty, heavy-footed, bent-kneed.

Flora, with the last of their luncheon, has made him a pie in a white dish. It is richly browned on the top and gives off a burnt and savoury aroma when she places it before him on the tea-table. But apart from this, apart from the delicious crispness of the potato crust and the smoothness of the creamed chicken within, the great charm of the pie lies in its being especially his own, and he eats it slowly, in small grateful mouthfuls. And when Nanny mentions that tonight is Flora's night off he begins to question her in a fondly authoritative fashion.

'What are you going to do, Flora?'

'I'm away to the whist-drive, Vere.'

'Where's the whist-drive?'

'At Long Cretton.'

'Are you going alone?'

'No.'

'Who are you going with?'

Flora looks at Nanny.

'But who are you going with, Flora? You must tell me.'

'Eat up your tea, Vere,' Nanny says.

'Will you win a prize, Flora?'

'I don't know.'

'But if you do win, will it be money?'

'Yes, I expect so.'

'Will it be as much money as Nanny will win if she gets the crossword right?'

'Good gracious, child,' says Nanny. Flora laughs.

'But honestly, will it?'

'No, sweetheart. If I did win I'd perhaps get thirty shillings.'

'Is that enough for us to keep ducks?'

Both Nanny and Flora laugh. To have made Nanny laugh is a feather in Vere's cap, and although he intended no joke, he begins to feel droll and amusing.

'If we kept ducks,' says he, 'we could fatten them up and sell them to Mummy and go away and live on the money. Couldn't we, Flora? We'd get married probably, and have lots of chickens and ducks, and sell them all to Mummy. We'd be quite rich, I expect. Wouldn't you like that, Flora?'

Laughter greets each sally. He does not understand why. His success amazes and delights him, he wants to go on being funny, but is not sure what new note to strike. He turns to traditional humour, raking up incidents which have been laughed at many times before: when Mrs Lark the cook for instance was seen to scratch her back with the long-handled soup spoon. But try as he will he cannot prolong the joke. Flora, who always cries when she laughs, starts to dry her eyes and Nanny advises him to finish his tea.

He does not mind. He is so well-pleased with himself that he eats several slices of bread and butter spread with honey in the comb, and drinks three cupfuls of milk straight off. Every so often he bursts into laughter, remembering his witty remarks, and he hums while he chews until Nanny stops him, and then blows bubbles in his cup. As soon as tea is finished he jumps from his chair and starts running round the nursery table. Each time he passes Flora, who is clearing the crockery away, he says either 'Hullo, sweetheart,' or 'Christmas is coming, the ducks are getting fat.' These phrases reduce him to such a state of uncontrollable laughter that he can hardly keep his feet and wobbles about like a drunken zany. Nanny, sitting with Faith on a low chair in front of the fire, tells him not to be silly: but this is only a fresh cause for merriment. His older sisters, dressed in blue school tunics, enter the room. They are going to play cards with Mal downstairs and are full of the doings of their day at school. Vere will hardly let them speak. He dances in front of them, his head cocked to one side, flapping his arms as if they were wings. The two girls look at him oddly, ask Nanny to make him stop and finally leave the room, shaking their heads. He bows them out, skips back to the sofa and turns two clumsy somersaults. Nanny warns him that it will all end in tears. Tears? What are they? Faith, watching him over Nanny's shoulder, grins encouragement. He falls onto the floor, makes faces, performs mad antics for her benefit. She screams and dribbles with amusement. He crawls to the chair by the window, racked with laughter, gripped and dissolved by it, as weak as water, almost incapable of movement, and struggles and sways and slips, hysterical and helpless.

Suddenly he stops.

Something dreadful, terrible, frightful has happened. He cannot believe it. He cannot even bear to verify his suspicions. He gives a small choking laugh, almost a sob, a mocking echo, and sits with his mouth clamped open.

'Nanny!' he wails without closing or in any way disturbing the wide set of his mouth.

Nanny turns to look at him. 'Whatever is the matter, Vere?'

'Nanny, Nanny!'

'What is it, child, for any sake?'

'My tooth!'

Nanny picks up the baby and comes across to him. 'Have you given it a bang, or what?' she says.

'I've lost it.'

'I can't understand you.'

He yells at her, using neither his lips nor his tongue: 'I've lost it, look!'

'You've lost it? But it's still there. I can see it.'

He moves his tongue a fraction of an inch. He tastes blood – there is blood on his tongue! Feeling cold all over he yells louder and more furiously, 'But it's come out, I tell you!'

Nanny laughs. How can she? And yet it is funny. He can see the funny side himself. Oh glory! What is he to do?

'Don't laugh, Nanny, don't!' he cries.

'Well, pull it out, Vere.'

'No!'

'But it's hanging by a thread.'

'No!'

'Well, shall I tie it to the door with a string?'

'Nanny!!'

'Vere now, don't be silly.'

'I'm not!'

'Well then, be brave.'

'I am, I am!'

'Go on and pull it out then. Let me pull it out.'

'No, no, no, no!'

'Yes, Vere, come here.'

'No! No! Nanny! Nanny!!'

Nanny is laughing, reaching down! He makes an abrupt dodging movement. Something falls onto the floor. What is it on the brown linoleum? He squints, trying to see. It is his tooth, his front tooth.

'Now you're not hurt, Vere, it just dropped out. What did I say? I knew all that carrying-on would end in tears. Don't be stupid, child, it's all over.'

Yes, but his tooth is on the floor; there is an empty space in his mouth which he dare not touch; he is afraid to swallow because of the taste of blood.

Flora enters the room. Nanny, walking up and down and patting the baby, tells her the story. Flora laughs, then kneels beside Vere who is still sitting rigidly in the chair.

'Let's have a look, sweetheart.'

'Here.' He raises his hand and points. 'Is it bleeding, Flora?'

'Oh yes, I see. Where's the tooth, Vere? You haven't swallowed it?'

'No, no!' How can she think of such things? 'Please, Flora, is it bleeding?'

'No. I don't think so.'

He closes his mouth gradually. The gap feels strange against his lips. He moves his head. The muscles in his neck are stiff and aching. He gets up and walks – or tries to glide at least –

over to the looking-glass. The sight of the empty socket makes him shudder.

'I thought he'd have to have it pulled by the dentist,' Flora is saying to Nanny. 'It's been loose I don't know how long.'

'Yes, it's a blessing, Vere. You ought to be grateful, instead of looking as if the end of the world had come.'

Impressed by this consideration Vere asks if he can see the tooth.

'Is it alive?' he questions Flora.

'No, sweetheart.'

'It's small, isn't it?'

'It's a milk-tooth, a baby-tooth.'

'Like Faith's?'

'Yes.'

'Shall I show it to Faith, Nanny?'

'What notions you do have, Vere. Yes, if you want, before I put her to bed.'

He takes the tooth gingerly between finger and thumb and exhibits it. To his surprise Faith is not interested.

'But look, Faith.'

'It's no good, she doesn't know what it is.'

'It's my tooth, Faith.'

'Kiss her goodnight, Vere, it's past her bedtime.'

'But it's my tooth. It's come out of my mouth. Faith, will you look!'

'Leave her alone, child, she doesn't understand.'

After Nanny and Faith have gone Vere sits with Flora on the sofa. The sun has moved round and the big low-ceilinged room is now in shadow. Looking at the tooth which reposes in the hollow of his hand, Vere is filled with morbid fascination, wonder and relief.

'It must have been pretty loose, mustn't it,' he remarks, 'because my lips aren't bruised at all.'

'You probably just caught it with your knee.'

'Why was it so loose do you think?'

'I expect you've another tooth coming.'

'In the same place? A baby-tooth?'

'No, a grown-up one.'

'To last forever?'

'Yes.'

'Until I die?'

'Now, Vere.'

'It was awful, Flora. I was laughing.'

Although he still shudders from time to time Vere's experience now seems to him both humorous and exciting; and the free, generous, confidential mood produced by it he would like never to end.

'Flora, have you eaten your Milky Way?'

'To tell you the truth I'd forgotten it.'

'I'd forgotten mine too. Shall we eat them now, together?'

'Yes, all right.'

He goes to the drawer in the dresser and fetches Flora's Milky Way. His own, he is afraid, having been in his pocket all day, will be broken and melted. But when he extracts it and his suspicions are confirmed, and Flora sees it and offers him hers, he refuses, saying that he likes his Milky Ways to be just so.

They sit side by side on the sofa, the girl's eyes dreamy and faraway, the boy eating slowly and with care, and converse quietly together. Vere asks questions to which he already knows the answers, wishing to perpetuate the perfect atmosphere, and Flora summons up her gentle voice in reply. The budgerigars twitter and flit about their cage, and the freshly-lit fire smoulders and smokes in the grate.

'Milky Ways are awfully milky, aren't they, Flora?'

'Does it hurt to eat, Vere?'

'Not really. I only use one side of my mouth, you see.' A pause. 'Aren't you pleased I thought of the Milky Ways? I'll buy you another tomorrow.'

'You mustn't, sweetheart.'

'Why?'

They study his tooth through Nanny's magnifying glass, and Flora tells him he must keep it to show his parents when they come to say goodnight. She says they may give him sixpence for it. When it is time for Vere to have his bath therefore, he runs ahead of Flora into the bathroom and polishes the tooth with his toothbrush until it shines: then he wraps it in cotton wool and puts it in a pill-box which she has found for him. After his bath he places the box beneath his pillow, says his prayers, gets quickly into bed and waits.

What can be detaining his father and mother? He considers how best to describe his ordeal. How curious and concerned his parents are going to be. He dwells pleasantly in his imagination on their amazement and anxiety. His father may judge his pain and suffering worth a shilling, his heroism worth two. Sweet vistas begin to open before him. If only they would come!

But his father, he suddenly remembers, went to play golf. He might not be back for hours! And his mother, where is his mother? He learns that she is fetching his father from the golf-course. Have they returned? Not yet. When will they return?

'Soon, sweetheart, I expect. You needn't go to sleep for a bit.'

He will not see them: they will not come in time: that is obvious. It is sad when he has so much to tell and to show them, when he has made such preparations. He might as well go to sleep – are those voices on the stairs? Of course not. It is foolish of him to strain his ears. He knows that they will not come: he is sure of it.

He starts to sing to himself. He has not seen his mother since he knocked on her bedroom door, kissed her across the breakfast-tray and asked her how she was: except once, he recalls, during the afternoon. She was in the garden, tying back the purple clematis with raffia, a basket with secateurs on the ground beside her and a large pink floppy straw hat on her head. He paused and watched her, taking pleasure in the sight. Her presence seemed to complete the sunlit peacefulness of the scene, her intricate operations to complement his own furious toil. He wishes . . . But no; he will wish no more. He notices that his song has assumed a form. He tries to recapture and repeat it, but it eludes him. Will they never come?

When he first hears the soft rubber footfalls on the nursery passage he smothers them with song because he thinks they are a trick of his imagination. But his mother's following steps are undeniable. He listens, catches a snatch of tuneless whistle, sits up in bed and calls.

His father says, bending his head as he comes into the room, 'Well, you monkey, what have you been up to?'

'Darling,' his mother says, going to sit on the rail of the fireguard.

Vere hides his excitement so well that his greeting sounds detached and cool.

'Have you had a nice time, darling?' his mother asks, smoking elegantly, while his father regards his reflection in the looking-glass on the cupboard-door.

'Yes, thank you, Mummy,' Vere answers, suddenly uncertain about the best way in which to approach the great subject, in which to claim his parents' interest. 'I've got something to tell you,' he starts.

'What's that, old boy?' says his father, not turning.

'Well, my tooth's come out. Here, this one, it was loose.' His words are conveying nothing, he senses it. What has become of his thrilling account? 'I was laughing, and I knocked it with my knee, and it came out,' he says.

'Why, so it has.'

'Oh yes, darling.'

'Open your mouth.'

'Was it terribly painful?'

'A bit,' he admits, feeling better.

'Are you all right now?'

'Oh yes,' he says impatiently.

'But it's horrid when you lose a tooth,' his mother continues. 'Did it bleed much?'

'Yes, a little . . .' Is it dangerous if your mouth bleeds, he wonders.

'You won't be able to whistle through your teeth,' his father says with a smile.

'You will when your new tooth grows, darling.'

'But would you like to see the old one?' Vere insists.

'Good God, have you got it in bed with you?'

His mother gives his father a nudge and says, 'Yes, darling, let's see it.'

He shows his mother and calls to his father, who has turned back to the mirror. 'Don't you want to see it, Dad?'

His mother says, 'Do come and look, David,' without looking herself.

'Here, Mummy.'

'Isn't it clean?'

'I brushed it.'

'Cleaner than your other ones are sometimes, I'm afraid, darling.'

'Yes . . .'

His father asks him what he is going to do with it.

'Well, I'm going to keep it.'

'What for?'

'Well, I don't know, I might sell it or something.'

'Sell it? Who to?'

'Oh, someone.'

'What a little rat you are.' A quacking noise. 'Is Faith asleep?'

'Faith? Yes, I think she is.'

'We ought to go down.'

'Oh don't go.'

His mother inquires if he would like his curtains drawn and his father wanders restlessly about the room. Vere regrets having asked them to stay. Nothing is happening as he expected, as he hoped, none of his lovely expectations being fulfilled.

'What is the time, David?'

'Well, it's after seven.'

'Perhaps we should go.'

'Come on, you cuddle down,' says his father, 'as snug as a bug in a rug.'

But Vere makes a final effort. 'Dad, don't you really think I'll be able to sell my tooth?'

'I shouldn't worry about it, old boy.'

'But I am worried.'

'Daddy might buy it from you if you ask him nicely. Go on, David.'

'That's all very fine. All right, all right. How much do you want for it?'

'I didn't mean I wanted to sell it to you.'

His father jingles the money in his pocket and produces a handful of change. 'What's the price?'

'No, honestly.'

'There's two-and-six. That's more money than I ever had at your age.'

'No, thank you, Dad.'

'Stop talking and take it, there's a good boy.'

'No, Dad.'

'I'd take it, darling.'

'No.'

He cannot accept the money now. Surely they can see that? It is unkind of his mother to shake her head, of his father to shrug and turn away. He has never, never wanted money – money alone. But he cannot explain. He lies back in bed and pulls the covers up to his chin.

'Is something the matter, darling?'

'No, Mummy . . .'

'Well then.'

'Going, going . . . gone! You are a silly boy. You'll never be rich. Come on, we're late.'

His mother leans over and kisses him and asks him if he will sleep. His father makes quacking noises and pinches his cheek.

'Goodnight, Mummy. Goodnight, Dad.'

'Goodnight, sleep tight, mind the fleas don't bite.'

Is the tooth so soon forgotten? Does his refusal of the half-crown and all that it entailed count for so little?

'Are you sure there's nothing wrong, darling?'

'No.' He smiles wanly.

'Well, goodnight then.'

'Goodnight, Mummy.'

'Dream of bunnies in the night.'

'Goodnight, Dad.'

'Goodnight, old boy.'

They go into the day-nursery. He can hear them speaking

to Nanny. Flora slips into his room, closes the door, comes and sits on his bed.

'What is it, Vere?' she asks.

'Have they been talking about me?'

'Your mother thinks you're looking sad.'

'I'm not.'

'What is it, sweetheart?'

'Nothing.'

'Let me put your pillow straight. Oh – did they give you a sixpence for your tooth?'

'No. But it isn't that, Flora. Daddy wanted to give me two-and-six, only I wouldn't take it.'

'Why though?'

'Well . . . I didn't want it.'

His parents' steps recede down the nursery passage and Nanny comes into his room.

'Vere, whatever have you been saying to your mother and father? They were quite worried.'

'It isn't my fault,' he answers. 'I haven't done anything.'

'I know what the trouble is with you. You're overtired. Look at the time. That's what it is, isn't it?'

'I am a bit tired,' he says, grateful for this simple explanation of the unhappy tightness at the pit of his stomach.

'Of course you are,' Nanny goes on, pulling down the blue blinds, and Vere believes her. 'You ought to be asleep. You're always like this when you're tired. I know you.'

And of course he is, it is perfectly true. He needs his sleep – he is a worker after all.

'Kiss Flora goodnight.'

'Goodnight, Flora.' He gives her such a hug that she nearly loses her balance.

'Vere!' She laughs. 'Goodnight, sweetheart.'

'Have a nice time.'

'I will.'

'And win the prize, Flora!'

'Are you thinking of our old ducks?'

Nanny says, 'Goodnight, Vere,' from the doorway.

'But Nanny,' he cries, 'aren't you going to kiss me goodnight?'

'Heavens, child, there's no end to it, is there? Goodnight, sleep tight.' She accentuates the words heavily, making a gesture with her hands as if to say; I suppose you think you won't be there for me to kiss tomorrow night, or the night after, or all the other nights.

'Tuck me in.'

'You are tucked in.'

'But my toes!'

'That's enough, Vere.'

'Goodnight, Nanny.'

She takes his head firmly in her hands and plants a kiss on his forehead.

'You will leave the door open?'

'Yes.'

'And you won't go away?'

'I may for a minute. I'm making no promises. Have you everything you want?'

'Yes, thank you, Nanny.'

'Well, go to sleep then, go to sleep.'

She half-closes the door, adjusts the stopper with her foot and turns on the day-nursery light. Flora patters down the passage. The budgerigars scold as they are covered up for the night. 'Goodnight, budgies,' Nanny says softly. 'Don't be afraid, you silly creatures, I'm not going to hurt you.' Even the birds seem subject to that effortless authority for they quieten immediately at the sound of her voice. Will she sit down and read by the fire? No; she is moving about, humming a hymn-tune, and now she is opening the other door, and now she is following Flora down the passage. Where is she going? Will she be long? Should he call? Anything can happen without her, Faith be ill or the house catch on fire. She ought not to desert him: she virtually promised . . . He will give her a minute before he calls.

He lies in bed and listens.

Out of doors the birds are singing. Would that be a blackbird beneath his window? Its song is still and clear. Rooks fly over the house. He can hear the weighty flapping of their wings as they head for their nests in the tall trees of the grove. The wheels of a farmcart grind along the drive, a whip cracks. Silence. The cooing of the white doves, sleepy and intimate, drifts from the crowded dovecotes. A late lark ascends from the buttercup field by the farm, and the swallows swoop shrilly on the insects of the hour. Soon the chill dimness will turn into night, full and blue. Bats will emerge squeaking from their secret haunts; owls will hoot; foxes bark; dew fall.

What is that?

Nanny is returning. Her steps weave down the passage, she enters the nursery, the springs of the sofa creak.

'Nanny?'

'Aren't you asleep yet, Vere?'

'Is everything all right?'

'Yes, yes, child. Close your eyes.'

'Goodnight, Nanny.'

'Goodnight, Vere.'

The boy turns over in his bed. He might have trusted Nanny: she would not let him down. She is next door, she will always be next door: her sure light will always shine: she will watch over him: he is safe forever.

The dusk blurs on blinds and curtains. Tomorrow . . . He hopes for fine weather. He has so much to do . . . Tomorrow . . .

TWO

THE BEE-STING

One morning Vere meets Mr White the milkman in the back-yard.

'Good morning, Mr White,' he says.

'Morning, young fellow-my-lad,' Mr White replies, as he kicks at the starter of his motorbicycle. 'You coming for a ride round to the garage?'

'Not today, thank you,' says Vere.

'Well, ta-ta for now.'

'Mr White!' Vere restrains him. 'Mr White, how does your motorbike work?'

'Can't stop now, young man. Jump on and see for yourself.'

'Round to the garage?'

'That's it.'

'I'll walk, Mr White, and then you can show me.'

'Not afraid, are you?'

'Afraid?' Vere laughs. 'I just want to walk.'

'Right you are!'

With a great rattling of the piled milk-bottles in the sidecar the machine rolls down the incline and roars round the corner.

Vere watches it out of sight, hears the gears change and the engine abruptly putter to a stop, and wonders what he should do. For many months now Mr White's morning visits have been a thorn in his flesh. He is possessed of a nagging and unfulfilled desire to take the milkman at his word. To ride on the motorbicycle, for however brief a spell, would be exciting, delightful, and also, he feels, a worthwhile experience. But Nanny, under threat of the severest penalties, has expressly forbidden him to do so.

Mr White of course does not know this. Receiving unchangingly polite refusals of his repeated and now challenging offers, he has not hesitated to draw his own conclusions and to state them. Thus Vere's pride has become involved in the matter, his courage has been called in question, and absurd though they are, it rests with him sooner or later to prove Mr White's suspicions false.

He sets off in the direction of the garage.

If he is to be perfectly truthful he has to admit that Nanny's attitude has raised a certain doubt in his mind. Is pillion-riding perhaps less simple than he imagines it to be? – That is the question. Is it in some unsuspected way difficult or dangerous? The mere idea of it perturbs Nanny: and although Mr White does not share her view and clearly ought to know best, Nanny is seldom wrong. Not that Vere is afraid. He wants to ride on the motorbicycle, he is really keen about it, and one day he will, even if it means taking his life in his hands.

The machine is parked by the henhouses. The boy approaches it and touches the controls on the handlebars. How frightful, he thinks, if I touched the wrong switch and the engine started and the whole affair shot down the drive. He withdraws his hand and begins to whistle. He picks up a stone, throws it at a telegraph-pole, then flashes round suddenly and punches the pillion-seat with his fist. It is shaped and spongy, he knows it of old: he could sit there in comfort and in safety, he is positive. He would mount by placing his right foot on the adjustable foot-rest – here: he clicks it down. Right foot on the rest – so, and the left leg thrown over. It is as easy as falling off a log. Then a firm and upright position and a good grip with the knees, as on a horse, and what harm could possibly befall him?

'Well, well, well! Coming for a ride after all?'

Vere starts. 'Oh, Mr White, I was trying the pillion,' he says. 'It's very springy, isn't it?'

'You wait till we get going.'

'What?' Vere starts to dismount. 'I was only trying it, Mr White.'

'No need to move, I can manage, stay where you are.' And laying a heavy hand on Vere's shoulder to balance himself the milkman poises his foot for the strong downward kick.

Vere is absolutely trapped. He bitterly regrets his actions of the last few minutes. 'Wouldn't it be easier if I got off, Mr White?' he asks.

'No no, that's all right,' Mr White replies as he bears down on the kick-start and twists the hand-throttle. The engine puffs a couple of times. 'I can manage fine,' he says.

'Can you really?' says Vere, feeling helpless and ill.

The engine roars.

'OK?' Mr White shouts, a broad grin on his frank fresh face.

'OK,' Vere answers, robbed by the rapid development of the situation of all power to protest.

Mr White snaps on a pair of goggles, shakes the wire milk-bottle frames in the sidecar, climbs over the petrol tank, sits down and calls, 'Mind you hang on now!'

'How? Like this?' Vere beseeches, clinging to the milkman's coat-tail.

'Arms round my waist.'

'Like this, like this?'

'That's the way,' sings out the milkman above the noise of the engine. 'Hold tight, off we go!'

The clutch engages, the motorbicycle moves, lurches round in a tight circle and then starts to splutter down the drive. When Vere opens his eyes he discovers with relief that he is hidden from the nursery windows by the garden wall. As long as no-one has seen him! But he cannot worry. The air is rushing through his hair and tousling it, the milkbottles are clinking merrily in the sidecar, the pillion-seat is even more comfortable than he expected. He screws up his eyes and peeps over Mr White's shoulder at the quickly-passing land-marks. There go the potting-sheds and the greenhouses. And here is Mr Bruise with a surprised expression on his face – and there, already, he is left behind. They must be touching fifty miles an hour. How intoxicating it is to speed along like this – it is worth anything – how right he was to accept the ride! He is a bird, a swift; he is borne on the wings of the air; he is flying through it, free, unhampered; he is gulping it into his lungs; he is feeling it tingle on his skin. He relaxes his hold of Mr White and cries, 'It's lovely.' He swings back in his seat and looks up at the sky. He grips with his bare knees and wishes he was going all the way to Long Cretton. He is light-headed with motion. 'It's lovely, Mr White,' he cries.

As they near the bottom of the drive they slow down. Vere is just beginning to feel disappointed when he becomes aware of a pricking sensation in his knee. It is probably the air, he thinks, the pressure of the air. But the slower they go the more insistent it grows, and when they stop he realises with dismay that it is not a pricking sensation any longer: it is a pain, and a pretty sharp one at that.

'How did you like it?' calls Mr White.

'Very much,' Vere answers, looking at his knee which has a round red spot on the inside.

'Well, hop off, young man, hop off. I must be getting along.'

'Mr White,' Vere says, dismounting, 'there's something wrong with my knee.'

'What's that?'

'I've got a pain in it.'

'You kept your knees turned out, didn't you?'

'No, I gripped, like riding. Ow, it is painful.'

'Well, you've gone and burnt yourself. That's what you've done.'

Horrorstruck, Vere says, 'Oh, Mr White, I haven't, have I?'

'That's what it is. A burn. And a nasty one too. You ought to have kept your legs well away from the exhaust pipes. They're bound to be hot, aren't they?'

'But I didn't know, Mr White.'

'Oh, never touch the exhausts,' the milkman says in the same tone that somebody might say: never jump out of windows.

'But what shall I do?'

'You rub some butter on it. That's the thing. All right?'

'Are you going?'

'Got to be on my way. You're all right though, aren't you?'

'I suppose so.'

'Well, ta-ta, young fellow-my-lad, ta-ta.'

'Ta-ta, Mr White.'

The milkman winks and grins, revs up his engine and disappears along the road.

Vere is most unhappy. He examines his burn and begins to hobble up the drive. His knee must have been sizzling against the exhaust pipe for ages, whilst he was pretending to be a bird et cetera. He might have known the ride would end in disaster. He was warned, and he never would have agreed to it except for Mr White; who forced him against his will to stick on the blessed motorbicycle – when he tried to get off – and who is therefore responsible for the burn! Oh yes, he attempted to prove it was Vere's fault, suggesting virtually Vere burnt his leg on purpose. No doubt, Vere thinks, he has burnt in his time many boys' legs and excused himself in the same way: he probably makes a habit of it. And leaving without any offer of help, without so much as a kind word or a thought for the consequences . . . The consequences, Vere repeats to himself with a shiver: and forgetting Mr White and his outrages he dwells with gloom and apprehension on the form that they are likely to take.

As he tops the rise by the greenhouses Mr Bruise catches sight of him and stops sweeping, and as soon as Vere is within earshot clears his throat and calls, 'Morning, Master Vere,' in a knowing manner.

Vere conceals his limp as best he can and answers, 'Morning, Mr Bruise.'

'I saw you, Master Vere.'

'Oh, did you?'

'I saw you on the motorbike. That's not allowed, is it?' And the old man winks a rheumy eye.

Vere is in no mood for winks and jokes and he says coldly, 'Yes, I saw you too.' He would like to ask Mr Bruise to keep his knowledge to himself, but because he feels that one should only ask favours of friends – and Mr Bruise's leering looks are not friendly at all – he maintains a haughty silence and passes on his way.

The gardener is not impressed. 'I saw you, Master Vere,' he crows with a grating laugh. 'You'll cop it. Wouldn't like to be in your shoes. Not half you're going to catch it – what a rumpus!'

Vere's heart sinks. His knee is really painful. The crimson circle has spread and the air burns and stings it horribly. He will have to go indoors. But then he will have to explain how he received the burn. And then he will catch it, as Mr Bruise so happily understated.

He must find Flora. It is his only chance: find her, tell her the truth and enlist her aid. Flora will help him, Flora will think of something. Flora is sweet and good and sympathetic; if Nanny will not understand, then Flora will. Where are you, Flora? he thinks. Flora, Flora, he says under his breath as he limps along in the shadow of the garden wall. Flora, Flora, he reiterates a hundred times, until the name loses its meaning and becomes a mere jumble of pained and fearful syllables. Flora, Flora, come and help me.

He skirts the backyard and calls softly up to the night-nursery windows. Receiving no response he goes round and stands beneath the day-nursery windows and calls.

'Oh Flora, Flora!'

Once he imagines he sees her behind the glinting panes. He waits for the window to be thrown up, for her head to appear, but nothing happens. He dare not raise his voice in case Nanny should hear him.

'Oh Flora.'

His knee is becoming more and more painful. He cannot postpone things any longer. He enters the house by the back-door, still calling for Flora, drags himself up the stairs and pauses at the top. If Flora is not alone in the day-nursery, if Nanny is there, then he is done for. He starts to tiptoe along the passage.

At the nursery door he stops and listens. All is quiet within. Perhaps Flora is darning. He opens the door a few inches.

'Who's that?'

Nanny's voice.

'It's me.'

'Oh, you gave me a fright, Vere. Well, come in or go out – make up your mind.'

'Nanny, I'm hurt.'

'For any sake.' She comes to his assistance. 'Where, child? What is it?'

Is she not angry, or even suspicious?

'It's painful,' he groans, playing for time and pointing to his knee. Somehow he expected her to know. If she does not, perhaps he might tell her a bit of the story, not everything at once? He could explain to Flora later, tell Flora the truth.

'Dear oh dear, it must be agony, child,' she says. 'How did you do it?'

'Don't touch it, Nanny!'

He racks his brains.

'I'm not touching anything. But how did you do it, Vere?'

'I was stung by a bee.'

'A bee?'

'Yes – ow, ow! By a bee, Nanny. It stung me – ow!'

'Come and sit down,' she says.

He has told not a half-truth but a black lie. It occurs to him and is out of his mouth before he can weigh it or restrain himself. If it is not accepted he is sunk.

'Tell me, Vere, now tell me. Have you taken the sting out?' She believes him.

'No.'

'Let me have a look. This is a funny sort of sting, Vere.'

'Why?'

'Well, it's all over red, and it's such an edge to it, and it's not much swollen.'

'I think it was a funny sort of bee,' he says.

'Whereabouts were you when you were stung?' she inquires, fetching her magnifying glass and peering through it to find the sting.

'Down the drive,' Vere answers.

'And what did the bee look like?'

'It was black and yellow, and furry, and big too.'

'Was it a wasp?'

'Oh no.'

'Well, I can't see any sting. Tell me what happened, exactly.'

'Well,' he pauses. 'I was walking down the drive. And suddenly the bee settled on my knee and I felt a terrific pain. I looked down and the bee was stinging me. It was as big as my thumb.'

'It must have been a queen bee.'

'I think it was.'

'Was there a swarm anywhere?'

'I don't know.'

'It's not like a bee to go and sting though. I can't understand it.'

'Well, this one did.'

'And what did you do, when you were stung?'

'I jumped. Nanny, it's painful. Won't you put something on it?'

'Vere, you're sure it was a bee and not anything else?'

'What else?'

Well, a horse-fly or something.'

'It was a bee, Nanny, I promise you.'

Deeper and deeper he commits himself: he is up to his ears in falsehood and deceit. He is amazed by himself and by Nanny's credulity. He feels faintly embarrassed at being able to practise so successfully on her trust, but he resolves that as soon as the pain is relieved he will make a clean breast of the whole affair.

Nanny says, poking about in the medicine cupboard: 'Where's that blue bag, let me think. I hid it somewhere for safety, and now I can't remember.'

'Nanny, do you put butter on stings?' he asks.

'Butter's for burns,' she answers.

'Oh, I see.'

'Well, here's some ammonia. I can't find the blue-bag, but ammonia's very good for stings, they say. Hold out your leg, Vere.'

'Will it hurt?'

'No, it'll be soothing. There. You poor boy, it is a bad place. There – is that better?'

She dabs his knee with a piece of cotton-wool soaked in the

liquid from the cloudy bottle. The smell of it is acid and stifling.
'How does it feel, Vere?'
'Worse.'
'It can't.'
'Much worse.'
'There's not something else in the bottle, is there? No.' She sniffs. 'It's ammonia all right.'
'Nanny!' The pain is becoming intolerable.
'You must be exaggerating, Vere.'
'Oh, what can I do? It's smarting, Nanny, it's smarting so.'
'Now, Vere.'
He cannot sit still. He jumps up and hops round the room.
'Come here and let me look at it again.'
'But it's dreadful, Nanny. I can't bear it!'
'Well then, come here!'
He runs back to the sofa and hurls himself about on it, gritting his teeth and butting his head against the cushions.
After a glance at his leg, which she has seized, Nanny exclaims, 'Good heavens, child, it's all over blisters!'
She sounds so worried that Vere pauses and looks at the leg himself. At this moment Flora enters the room.
'Flora,' Vere moans, 'my leg's all blisters. Where have you been?'
There is a puzzled and doubtful expression on Flora's face. 'I've been collecting some watercress down the garden,' she says. 'I saw Mr Bruise. Oh Vere, what have you been doing?'
'Flora, will you come and look at this sting on his knee,' says Nanny. 'I can't make it out.'
'Sting?' asks Flora.
'Yes, he was stung by a bee.'
'Were you, Vere?'
'Mmm,' he says, not liking actually to enunciate the lie a second time, for he knows that the game is up, he knows that Flora knows.
'Why are you smiling?' Nanny asks. 'It is a bee-sting, isn't it?'
'It is a sting,' he answers, 'in a way. It's a sort of sting. You see, I was stung by the exhaust pipe of Mr White's motorbike.'

'What are you saying, Vere, what do you mean? This isn't a burn?'

'Yes, it is, sort of.'

'A burn? And I put ammonia on it? Oh child, child. Go down and fetch his mother, Flora.'

'No, Nanny,' Vere says.

'Quickly, Flora, and tell her it's urgent.'

Flora goes: Nanny rummages in the medicine cupboard: Vere sits fearfully on the edge of the sofa. Nanny's consternation and now her threatening silence, the unwonted summoning of his mother, the pain in his leg and the dire consequences he imagines will result from the application of the ammonia – all these things terrify him. He starts seriously to regret his lies. But when his mother arrives she is full of sympathy, and also, he notices, secretly amused by the story he has told. She asks him questions as she dresses his knee, her touch deliciously deft and gentle, and looks once or twice as if she is going to laugh out loud. This makes him think of the lie less as a crime and more as something excusable, jolly and sly. Of which he is the victim after all he argues, when, a trifle resentfully, he meets Nanny's glum forbidding gaze.

He manages not to wince during his mother's operations and is congratulated on his courage, though his knee is now only numb. Flora shakes her head and clicks her tongue a certain amount, and his mother says, fastening the bandage with a safety-pin, 'Well, darling, let this be a lesson to you not to tell lies': but Vere, reflecting what seems to be the view of the majority, cannot feel unduly depressed. His ruse has fulfilled its intended function – and it was a ruse, he insists to himself as he meets Nanny's eye a second time.

His mother helps him to his feet and supports him when he tries to walk. He leans heavily on her arm, determined to make the most of her in this much-loved rôle, and suggests that they venture farther afield. Leaving Nanny to tidy the nursery they go along the passage and down the stairs, and find Vere's father in the hall. On being told what has taken place he smiles, his eyes crinkle and he calls Vere a monkey.

'Would you like to walk a little in the garden, darling?'

'Oh yes, Mummy, please.'

Together they stroll over the lawns, along the paved paths and between the yew-hedges.

'What did you say the bee was like, darling?'

'I said it was covered with fur, like a dog.'

'How big did you say it was?'

'Awfully big. And I said it had nine legs.'

'Good God.'

'And a sting like a knitting-needle.'

'Darling!'

'I did.'

'And Nanny believed you?' asks his father.

For some reason that he does not understand Vere pauses. 'She must be mad,' his father comments.

'Well, I made it all sound true.'

'You must have had a job.'

'Well, yes,' Vere laughs, and continues to give extravagant replies to the questions he is asked.

After several circuits of the lilypool his mother says that it is time for luncheon. With a light heart Vere bids his parents goodbye, hobbles to the gate in the garden wall, and then, screened from their sympathetic view, walks briskly into the house and up to the nursery.

He is unpleasantly surprised during the meal by Nanny's accusing looks and curt rejoinders; they slightly damp his carefree mood; but judging it only a matter of time before she sees the funny side of the events of the morning, he refuses to pay any great attention. When she declines to read to him after luncheon however, saying he does not deserve it, he considers she is carrying her disapproval too far and feels slighted, hurt, then angry. He tells himself she is humourless, obstinate, stuck-up, stupid and unfair. He does hope, all the same, that matters will have improved by tea-time.

At teatime, if anything, they are worse. Although Vere makes one or two attempts at conversation most of the meal passes in silence. He leaves the nursery as soon as he is able, furiously resolving not to let Nanny's displeasure upset him, and seeks distraction out of doors. But he can find nothing to absorb or even occupy him: he wanders about the garden, idle and disconsolate, for an hour: and when the curfew is rung from the nursery window is still trying to persuade himself that her behaviour is unreasonable.

His mother arrives to rebandage his knee before he goes to bed. The burn, exacerbated by the ammonia, is raw and sensitive. On impulse, as a peace offering, in consideration of the blame that he knows Nanny assumes for its condition, he minimises his discomfort. But her steely glances show no sign of softening: and after healing anodynes have been applied, the pain has been eased and his mother has laughed again at his account of the morning's adventures, the spirit of rebelliousness once more flares within him.

This feeling persists – he clings to it at least – until Nanny comes into his room later in the evening, carefully closes the day-nursery door and subjects him to a long and searching scrutiny. He has been sitting up in bed, singing with revolutionary if uneasy vigour. His song weakens as she crosses and sits on the end of his bed, and when she asks if he has anything to tell her, suddenly dies.

'Well, have you, Vere?' she repeats.

'No, I haven't,' he answers, marshalling his forces and giving her stare for stare.

'Are you sure, Vere?'

'Yes.'

She tries a flank attack. 'I want you to think what you did this morning.'

He goes to meet it. 'Nothing. I didn't do anything.'

'That's not the truth,' she says, bearing down on him. 'What did you do?'

'I rode on the motorbike.'

'I know, but I'm not speaking of that. What else?'

'Nothing else.'

'You told me a lie.'

'Oh Nanny!' He essays a laugh – for it is laughable, this mountain she is making out of a molehill. 'It was a fib.'

'It was a lie, and why did you tell it?'

'All right, I'm sorry,' he says abruptly and looks away, not beaten yet.

'That's not the way to say you're sorry and look at me, please,' she says. 'You told me a lie to get out of your punishment for riding on the motorbicycle, when you were forbidden – that's why you told it me.'

'But it was funny,' he exclaims.

'I think it was cowardly, Vere. I do.'

He repudiates the charge without conviction. Before he has time to collect himself she thrusts home her advantage.

'And I didn't expect it of you. I'm afraid you're not the boy I thought you were.'

'I am, Nanny,' he says, pressing back against his pillows and regarding her with round and nervous eyes.

'Another thing, Vere.' What now, he wonders, gathering his deflated forces together. 'I believed you, I believed your lie, and you set me up as a laughing-stock in front of your mother and father.'

'Oh Nanny, no.'

'Yes, Vere. Laughing like you did, because I believed you – it was inconsiderate and thoughtless and unkind.'

'Oh Nanny, please,' he whispers in surrender. His position collapses: it was always undermined. His strength ebbs away in his guilt, which he has felt but not till now comprehended. He is defeated.

'Well, Vere, goodnight,' Nanny says.

He has imagined his defeat was total: he has expected peace. Now he discovers his mistake. A truce is still war. Peace without reconciliation he cannot endure.

'You can't go!' he cries; and in his quick unhappiness he sees at last the real error of his ways, understands of a sudden how he has made her suffer, knows that he has been in truth unfeeling, heartless.

'I can do as I like,' she answers, rising to her feet.

In the light of his unhappiness he understands that too. She is free and independent, for he has severed – severed unthinkingly – the bonds of love, of respect and trust, which linked them. Clearly he perceives the tenderness of friendship

– the risks and dangers of each careless word, each unweighed action. But if she will not leave him now – if only she will stay – how he will prove his love!

'Nanny, please don't go,' he says, and holds her square hands tightly in his own. 'I didn't mean to laugh. I won't again. I thought it was funny. I didn't know. I won't tell any more lies. I promise you. I do see now. I'm very sorry. Only don't go, Nanny, not like that.'

She sits on his bed. 'Now child, there there,' she says. 'I'll stay a minute. Don't cry, I know when you're sorry. We'll let bygones be bygones. Dry your eyes, here's my handkerchief.'

He takes her handkerchief and blows his nose. A pent-up flood of warm relief, of thankfulness, of love, courses and sweeps throughout his being. Kneeling beside his bed he says his prayers.

'Oh Nanny.'

He hugs and kisses her goodnight.

'There, child, it's forgiven and forgotten.'

'I'm going to be really good after this.'

'We must all try.'

'Always though.'

'It's not easy.'

'I don't mind.'

'Goodnight, my boy.'

'Goodnight, Nanny.'

THREE

HOUSES AND A BOOK

Vere's first house was no more than a nest, hollowed out of the tall grass bordering the drive, into which he used to leap from a distance so as to leave no tell-tale trodden path, and from which he could spy secretly on the garden, the lawns and the front-door. Crouching there by the hour, eaten alive by ants, midges and harvest-bugs, only his hair and forehead showing between the waving stalks, he would wait patiently for the reward of unsuspecting steps or the rare delight of an overheard conversation. His nest was not enduring. One morning he was lying in it on his back, gazing through the clean branches of the beech trees at the blue sky above, when he became aware of a recurrent and rhythmical scraping sound that set his teeth on edge. He rolled over and scanned the horizon. Old Harris, the gardener, not ten yards away, was sharpening the curving blade of his scythe with a whetstone. As soon as Vere heard the close and regular rush of the blade, laying the grass – the very walls of his house – in wide semicircular swathes, he jumped to his feet. Harris dropped the scythe, opened his mouth, told him to clear off. Convinced by the gardener's anxiety that he had had a narrow shave, Vere did as he was told. Revisiting the scene later in the day he was unable to discover the exact position of his nest. The grass was uniformly short and tufty, and landmarks like twigs and stones had been removed. He regretted his loss, then he forgot it. Such was the seed of later enterprise.

But that was long ago, the previous summer. Winter comes. Crude shelters begin to appear about the place, branches resting against the trunk of a tree or a piece of rusty corrugated-iron enclosing the angle of a wall – shelters constructed in an hour or two and hardly occupied as long. Christmas passes, and the holidays with their interruption of Vere's activities. Alone again he idly thinks of houses, awaiting some sign, some impetus. One winter's evening, when the wind howls round the corners of the house and the cowl on the nursery chimney moans and whistles, he receives it.

Nanny, after offering to read to him, searches in the bookshelf and takes down a thick-leafed volume entitled *Settlers in Canada.*

'Has it any pictures?' he asks.

'No, but it's a nice book just the same. Come and sit down.'

'Can I see it?'

'You ought to read to yourself. You read quite well, Mademoiselle was saying.'

'No, you read, Nanny. But this looks awful. Couldn't we have Little Jack Rabbit?'

'I've read Little Jack Rabbit till I'm sick of it,' she says. 'You must know it by heart. Besides, a big boy like you – you're too old for Little Jack Rabbit. We'll try this one. Pull up to the fire and listen.'

'Can I have a marshmallow first?'

'They're in the top drawer, Vere. And you might fetch me a peppermint while you're there.'

'I've brought you two peppermints, Nanny.'

'Oh, very well. Thank you, Vere. Now.'

Clearing her throat and sucking on the peppermint, Nanny reads: '*Settlers in Canada.* Chapter One.'

The first chapter is not long and concerns a noble English family which, somehow disinherited, decides to emigrate to the New World. At the end of it Nanny inquires if she shall continue. 'Please,' Vere answers, happily nibbling his damp marshmallow and feeling the heat of the fire on his face.

In the second chapter the settlers arrive in Canada, penetrate into the virgin country and search for a site on which to build their home.

And from this point onwards Vere ceases to nibble. He swallows the marshmallow, forgetting to chew it properly or to lick his fingers, and heedless of the interesting outdoor noises, starts to attend in earnest. For these people in the story, without professional experience and with only limited and natural resources, are about to build themselves a house, a fastness capable of resisting both the weather and attack, in a strange and trackless countryside from which they will have to wrest their livelihood. The significance of it all, like rain in a dry summer, transforms his landscape. It is this, precisely this, for which he has been waiting. It is the sign, the revelation. He too will sally into the wild country; he too will build himself a strong house; he too will live by the sweat of his brow. The example of the settlers fires him with unconquerable enthusiasm. He wants to begin at once, this evening. His teeth chatter with zeal and excitement.

'Oh Nanny, read that bit again!'

'Which bit?'

'The bit where they start building their house.'

'I've read it once.'

'Yes, but again.'

'Do you like it, Vere?'

'Yes, I do!'

The words are like fairy gold which he can harvest and glean at his leisure, leaving no speck behind, and treasure ever after. Or they are like some magical solution transmuting the dross of vague unformulated longings into the precious gold of a clear object, an aim. Either way they are gold – they shed a golden light on present and future – gold unalloyed, priceless, glittering.

Nanny reaches the end of the second chapter and the time comes for Vere to go to bed. He runs into the bathroom, taking the book with him, washes, cleans his teeth, puts on his pyjamas, dashes back to the night-nursery and is reading by his shaded bedside lamp – all within three minutes.

The settlers decide to build their house by the banks of a broad and tree-lined river. A great plain opens around them, fringed by a distant forest. Receiving help from the soldiers of a fortress situated some miles down river, they build first of all a stockade as a protection against the Indians and packs of fierce wolves that infest the countryside. Surrounded by threats and dangers, in an atmosphere of trust and reliance, they work without pause through the sweet summer days, felling the forest trees and setting up the saw bench, jointing the broad stakes for the stockade and laying the foundations of the house, constructing a yard and outbuildings for the animals.

Vere has just finished the third chapter when Nanny comes to say goodnight. He feels full, as if he has eaten a large meal and needs time to digest it, and is therefore not sorry.

'What a lot you've read, Vere!'

'Yes, I've read a whole chapter.'

'Goodness gracious.'

'It is a tremendous lot, isn't it?'

'You must like the book.'

'I do.'

'Goodnight, Vere.'

'Goodnight, Nanny.'

While the wind batters against his windows and the farm-dog from its cold kennel faintly bays the fleeting moonlight, Vere lies in his warm bed, thinking disconnectedly. When he moves he notices that he aches slightly all over and his muscles are tense, as if from much exertion. The settlers slept under the stars, he thinks, the roar and eddy of the river filling their ears, the smoke from camp fires rising into the night. But not in winter, he recalls. He curls up and shuts his eyes. Still he sees the wide Canadian plain and the great trees. Like the settlers he is a breaker of new ground, a pioneer. He also belongs and does not belong; he also will build a house, a place of his own. And there he will live, lapped by Nature, resisting and loving it, forever contented, forever hardworking, self-reliant and admired. He falls into a dreamless sleep.

Waking in the morning refreshed he restrains himself with

an effort from setting to work immediately. Instead, judging he can gain more from a quick but thorough study of the settlers' methods, he reads intently through the succeeding days.

The first snows of winter hold off until the homestead is ready. Then, with the gates of the stockade closed and the beasts in the byre, and with all sounds deadened by the softly descending flakes, the settlers resign themselves to the enforced inactivity and isolation of the cold season. They are not idle: furniture has to be made, animals have to be cared for. Nor are they dull: one night, in the middle of a frightful blizzard, starving wolves break into the stockade. But at length the ice on the frozen river is swept away, the water begins once more to flow and to gurgle and the tireless work is resumed.

The story develops. A friendly Indian is introduced, complete with wigwam and blanket. Then the youngest settler, a little girl, is abducted by a party of marauding braves. A chase ensues. The settlers, the Indian and the soldiers from the fort track down the culprits, and after desperate expedients – the climax of the book – rescue the child. Finally the settlers inherit their rightful English property and title, and prepare to leave Canada.

Over the tea-table on the afternoon that he finishes the book Vere discusses it with Nanny and Flora.

'Well, did the settlers save little Rosemary?' Nanny asks as she pours the tea, having heard at luncheon that the child was missing.

'Yes, they saved her all right,' he answers.

'I'm glad to hear it.'

'How did they manage?' Flora inquires. When he has explained she says, 'It must have been exciting.'

'Yes, it was,' he admits, meaning, Not nearly so exciting as the building of the house.

Nanny says, 'And what happens in the end, Vere?'

'The father becomes a Lord – he is one really all the time – and he's awfully rich, so the settlers come back to England.'

'Well, that's very nice,' Nanny observes.

Vere munches thoughtfully, then asks, 'Why do you suppose they want to leave Canada?'

'They've inherited the money and the name, and they have their place to keep up – it's quite natural,' Nanny explains.

'But they're happy in Canada, aren't they?' he reasons. 'Why should they want to leave?'

'Perhaps they don't like it, sweetheart, not really.'

'Oh but they do! It's lovely there.'

'It's a hard life, Vere.'

'Yes, I know,' he says, uncomprehending. For it is exactly the hard life that he finds so attractive. The settlers have not been making the best of a bad job in Canada: they have been engaged in an enviable and inspiring work. Is it possible that they can wish to exchange their freedom for money, titles, places in England?

'Of course they'll not be happy, will they,' he says, 'when they get back, I mean?'

'Why not, Vere?'

'Well – they won't have anything to do, a house to build or anything.'

'I expect that's why they're returning. They don't want all that bother and nuisance a second time.'

'Bother, Nanny?'

'No.'

'Eat your cake, sweetheart.'

He begins to feel depressed. If Nanny is right, then all that he has loved in the story is meaningless.

'I'm sure they won't be happy,' he says. 'Not in the same way.'

'It's only a book, Vere, remember.'

'Well, they won't be happy. I know they won't.'

He denies the settlers happiness. If they regard the wonder of their life in Canada as no more than a nuisance, they will have to pay for their mistake with a sorrowful future. He commits them to misery and feels much better.

'How long did it take you to read the book?'

'Four days,' he answers, diverted by Flora's question.

'And you read it all yourself?'

'Yes.'

'Most of it, Vere.'

'Most of it I read by myself.'

Soon after this the rough March weather changes. The days are quiet and misty, and the trees drip although no rain falls. Vere gives up worrying about the complications of the settlers' story. He has his essential treasure, he cares for nothing else. With a knapsack containing biscuits and string over his shoulder he starts looking for a site on which to build his house. He combs the countryside, keen-eyed, heavily trudging, poking into unlikely parts of the garden and the grove of trees. Eventually, in the undergrowth behind the tennis-court, he finds his ideal situation. On the first sunny day in April the work is set in motion.

He has chosen the angle formed by two walls for his purpose. The property is squared off by willows and evergreens on one side, which screen him from overlooking windows, and by the corroded iron wheels and splintered wood of a disused water-pump on the other. There are empty outbuildings nearby which he can plunder, and an untended path, winding away from the pump and through the grove of trees, leads up to the terrace. Since the floor-planks of the old summer-house on the terrace are rotten and easily dislodged, this path is not without its uses. But he is careful on his journeys not to crush the nettles and sturdy weeds that surround his house, protecting it from chance discovery.

So begins for Vere a period of activity the like of which he has never known. His heart pulses with a steady and productive excitement. He is stronger and more resourceful than ever before. He glories in the size of his undertaking and the problems that confront him. His entire energy is concentrated on the project, every spare moment devoted to a form of toil connected with it. He can think of nothing else. Ideas come to him at meals or in his bath: he forgets to eat, to wash himself. Too absorbed to notice his happiness, too young to measure its depth, he works without respite.

Flora sometimes asks, 'When can we come and see your house?'

Pleased yet oddly not pleased by the question he usually parries it, saying either 'What?' or 'I'm deaf in that ear, Flora.'

'When are you going to let us come and see?'

'Oh, soon. Not long now.'

'Where is it, Vere?'

'Don't you know?'

'I don't.'

'Honestly?'

'I promise.'

Indulging himself he says, 'Where do you think, Flora?'

'I couldn't say.'

'Have a guess.'

'Round by the chickens?' He shakes his head. 'In the wood-shed?'

'Indoors?' he exclaims. 'No, Flora, it's miles from there if you want to know, miles and miles. I'm afraid you couldn't guess.'

'I said I couldn't.'

'But I'll give you one more try if you like.'

'It's no use, Vere.'

'You probably think it's in the garden, or behind the tennis-court, don't you, Flora?'

'It must be in one of those places.'

'Do you think so?'

'Where else could it be?'

'Well, it's not behind the tennis-court. Fancy you thinking it's there! You'll have to wait and see, won't you?'

'I don't think I can much longer.'

At the time these conversations induce feelings of elation and superiority, but afterwards he regrets them. They leave a boastful and unpleasant taste in his mouth. Although he longs to broadcast the tale of his triumphs, the least word that he lets slip causes him a pang as of betrayal. He does not understand his contrary emotions until one afternoon, passing the front-door with his star piece of material – the sheet of rusty corrugated-iron – balanced unsteadily on his head, he happens to meet his father.

'Hullo, Dad,' he says, lowering the iron with difficulty onto the paving and already, without knowing why, regretting the encounter.

'What the hell have you got there?' asks his father.

'It's a piece of corrugated-iron.'

'I can see that.' Vere's mother emerges from the front-door and his father says, 'I thought I was seeing things. Vere was carrying that damn great piece of iron.'

'Darling! You'll cut your fingers to ribbons! Leave it there and the gardeners will fetch it.'

'My fingers are all right, Mummy.'

His father inquires, 'Where on earth did it come from?'

'Yes, darling, where did you find it?'

'Oh, I've had it for years,' claims Vere.

'But really, you mustn't just take things,' his mother says.

'I haven't taken it. It's mine. The gardeners gave it me ages ago.'

'Well anyway, you'll have to let somebody help you.' As an afterthought his mother asks, 'What do you want with it?'

'What?'

'What do you want it for?'

'I'm building something.'

'What are you building?'

He pauses and says, 'Well, it's a house. I've built lots of houses but this is a better one, much better. Will you come and see it when it's finished?'

'I don't think you'll need that bit of iron though, will you, darling?'

He raises his voice, wondering if she has heard him. 'It's for my house, it's for the house I'm building.'

'Well, go very carefully – promise?'

'Yes, Mummy,' he says. 'You will come and see my house?'

'I can't today, I'm afraid.'

'No, when it's finished?'

'Another day, darling, yes.'

'And you will, Dad?'

'Yes, but for God's sake mind out with that iron.'

Vere shoulders his burden, trying not to show how unbearably heavy he actually finds it, and stumbles away.

To begin with he is furious with himself for having risked the front of the house; then he is saddened by his parents' reaction; finally he realises that he must not speak of what is closest to his heart. No-one can share his excitement: no-one believes in it, in his house or in him. But one day they will. Until his house is finished – only till then – he is on his own.

Day by day meanwhile, notwithstanding setbacks, the work advances. The stones on the top of the walls are rearranged, levelled and packed with earth. The planks from the summer-house are laid across to make a triangular shelter. This is so low that he excavates the soil, to the depth of about a foot, beneath it. The planks do not fit, their crumbling edges admit the light, and he begins to throw the excavated soil onto the roof. It falls through the gaps quicker than he can throw it. He fetches newspaper and spreads it over the planks. The soil after that remains pleasingly in position: he throws it up by the trowelful: it becomes a mountain. He would like to climb onto the roof to smooth it, but the planks sag alarmingly and he does not dare. At least no chinks of light remain: and when trees and bushes grow on the mountain, how secret his house will be – a sort of natural cavern!

The corrugated-iron – the largest part of the outside wall – he fixes against the roof, filling in at the sides with more planks. Over everything he then drapes sacks, wedging branches against them and driving in stakes for greater strength and solidity. He also hangs a sack above the narrow entrance to serve as a door.

The house inside is damp, pitch-dark and musty. By the light of a candle which he has borrowed from the cupboard in the pantry, he pats down the earth in the well of the floor and fashions a doorstep. He drives wooden pegs into crevices in the stone walls, for his coat and for tools, and makes an insecure shelf on which to keep stores such as candles and matches and biscuits.

Discovering that he can only stand upright in the very corner of the angle formed by the two walls – elsewhere the sag of the ceiling prevents it – he arranges a seat with a plank and some stones. Leaning right forward, in order not to collapse the outside wall, it is possible to sit there – it is really quite comfortable.

Three days after his eighth birthday he surveys his work.

The earth on the roof has settled down and already one or two weeds are sprouting. The thick wall of iron, planks, branches and sacks scarcely moves when he touches it. The floor of his house is level and hard, his knapsack and tools hang from the pegs. He climbs onto the water-pump. Beyond his house stretch fields and distant woods. The sun is shining on the wide landscape, but the corner of it that he has conquered and made his own is in shadow. He turns and edges through the nettles.

'Where have you been, Vere?' Nanny asks when he comes in late for tea. 'Didn't you hear the bell?'

'My house is finished,' he answers.

Flora enters the room and is told the news.

'Can we see it this evening, Vere?'

'Not till tomorrow,' he says. 'I've still one or two things to do.'

'Are you pleased with it?'

'Quite.'

'House,' says Faith.

'You can come too if you like, Faith.'

'House,' she repeats.

The rest of the evening is spent in a ferment of excitement. Vere is restless and talkative. Every conversation seems to wind up with a reference to his house. He tries without success to speak and to think of it calmly: he changes the subject a dozen times: the result is always the same.

Before going to bed he slips between the night-nursery curtains, and resting his forehead against the cool window-pane, looks out at the night. So much depends on the weather. Another clear day, he prays. If without sun, let it at least be dry and balmy. No rain, he pleads, no rain.

He sleeps fitfully. Waking with the first light he gets up and goes again to the window. The sky is overcast, there is a gusty wind. It may change, he thinks, it is still early. But by breakfast a light drizzle is falling. Nanny says it cannot last. He wants to believe her: yet how grey the sky is – no blue anywhere! As long as there is not a downpour. If necessary a drizzle, but please, he implores, please, please, no downpour.

The downpour comes at eleven o'clock. Vere is with Mal: this is the time, during his break, when she was to pay her promised visit.

'But after luncheon, chéri, we will go.'

'It'll be raining.'

'Then tomorrow.'

'It was all arranged for today, Mal. Everything was ready.'

'I know.'

The rain streams down. One hour, two hours pass. The sky is shrouded. Millions of drops of rain like sharp spears pierce and mutilate Vere's tender hopes. Wistfully he looks through the windows, mourning and grieving: and when Nanny at luncheon says that she thinks it is brightening, he smiles sarcastically and does not even bother to turn in his chair.

But Nanny is right. By two o'clock the clouds have lifted and beams of watery sunlight catch and silver spatters of late raindrops.

'Put on your wellingtons, Vere,' she says. 'You can fetch Mademoiselle on your way down.'

'Do you think it's worth trying to go?' he asks, anxious not to suffer fresh disappointment.

'Of course it is.'

'But the whole place'll be sopping wet.'

'Well, if it is, it is.'

'But you do understand, Nanny?'

'No, I don't understand,' she says. 'Stop worrying and put on your coat. We'll be out in a jiffy.'

'You don't know where to go, do you?'

'Yes, we do.'

'You do? Who told you?'

'A little bird. Run along.'

She hustles him out of the nursery. What little bird, he wonders as he walks along the passage. How can she know or think that she knows? He descends the staircase slowly, unable to ponder properly because of the revival of his vivid hopes, and finds Mal in the schoolroom wearing her soft raincoat and green hat with the jay's feathers.

'But you're all dressed,' he exclaims.

'I am dressed for the visit to your house,' she says. 'Can Scamp come with us?'

'She might as well.'

He leads the way through the side-door, feeling with every step more nervous and unwilling. He has made so much of his house: now he remembers a hundred faults in its construction, recalls that the job is not complete. It occurs to him that the rain may have injured some part of it, may even have destroyed the whole. And he does not know: what then is he doing? He warns Mal not to expect too much, blaming the weather for whatever deficiencies they may find. Mal says only, 'We will see.' He dislikes this answer, begins to feel that the expedition is being forced upon him, wishes he had never mentioned his house to anyone, hopes for more rain.

They reach the willows.

'Through here, Mal,' he says breathlessly.

She stumps forward, poking with her stick, and says, 'I can't go through there. It is too thick, Vere.'

'Yes, you can.'

'No, chéri.'

'Well, come round to this side.'

Trembling with controlled impatience, with excitement and uncertainty, he brushes through the undergrowth and climbs onto the water-pump. His house is still standing. It looks so natural and hoary with its branches and damp sacks and mountain of earth on top, as if it had stood there, in its concealed neglected corner, for all of time, that a sudden wave of relief and affection surges over Vere at the sight of it.

'Mal, here!' he cries, jumping down from the pump. 'You can get through easily!'

'But it is thrilling!' she says.

'Can you manage?'

'Mais oui.'

'There's my house, Mal.'

'Where?'

'There.'

The large woman and the boy, surrounded by the dripping trees, halt together at the edge of the open space. The warmth of the sun makes the earth steam around them. For a few seconds they gaze at the house in silence, then Vere says shakily, 'Mal, you see, it's only rough. I've hardly started on it yet. I just thought you might like to visit it sort of halfway – it's about half-finished.'

'It's lovely,' she says.

'It may be one day.'

'But now.'

'Do you think it is?' He cannot help smiling.

'Mais oui, mais oui! Lovely!'

She is speaking in her businesslike voice, she means what she says.

'How did you do it, Vere?'

It is this – the astonished question, the admiring glance, the unfeigned earnest interest – it is this for which he has slaved. By means of this house which he has created from nothing with his lonely labour, by means of this lasting expression of his deepest, strongest and best-loved mood, he has made his mark, he has gained his prize. Troubled no longer by fear or anxiety, his personality enlarged by his sweet success, he feels new powers stirring within him, unbreakable resolves, noble intentions.

'Tell me, how did you do it?'

'It took me a long time.'

'How long?'

'Weeks. Three weeks.'

'That is not long.'

'I worked awfully hard.'

'Amazing. Explain it to me. What are these sticks?'

'Sticks? That's the stockade.'

'I see.'

'I'm going to grow food here.'

'What sort of food?'

'Radishes and carrots.'

'And the house?'

'I'll show you. This is the door, this sack. Now you see these nails in the wall? I can fasten the door to whichever I want. For cold weather, or warm, or hot.'

'What made you think of such things?'

'That's nothing. Come in, Mal.'

Vere is so proud and happy. There are some beads of moisture on the ceiling planks, but the floor is almost dry. The house must be remarkably well-built to have withstood such an onslaught of wind and rain. And the faults? Why, he will put them right another day.

'Come in,' he calls.

'I can look from here, chéri.'

'But Mal, I've made you a seat. You must come right in.'

'I think I am too big for the door.'

'No, you're not,' he says, although she does seem enormous – her head alone completely blocks the doorway. 'Wait a second and I'll light the candle. There, that's better. Come on, Mal, you'll get in easily.'

'But chéri, I don't want to knock anything down.'

'You couldn't. It's tremendously strong. You see the step, don't you? Entrez.'

'Merci, Monsieur.'

She places one foot on the step and heaves her shoulders through the aperture.

'That's fine,' Vere encourages her. But Mal begins to laugh. 'What are you laughing at?'

'Eh bien, chéri – I am stuck.'

'No, Mal, you're not.'

'I am!'

'Where?'

'My hips.'

'Put your other leg in.'

'That is the leg with the rheumatism. I cannot move it an inch.'

'Try, Mal.'

'Quelle horreur!'

Whenever she laughs the drops of water on the ceiling shiver. Vere wishes she would not; there is nothing humorous in the situation; for both of them it is plainly becoming serious.

'No, Mal, please,' he says, 'try and move. You must now. Please, Mal. Are you ready? There!'

She enters the house. The entire structure rocks as she does so and little remains of the doorstep, but at least she is in. Bent double, refusing to sample the seat, saying that if she did she would never get up again, her face in the candlelight looking red and hot, she is none-the-less appreciative. Although he can scarcely move, Vere points out the various pegs in the walls and describes their uses, and recovering gradually from the shock he received when Mal stuck in the doorway, begins once more to glow and exult.

'It is all right, Mal, isn't it?'

'Really, I congratulate you.'

'Do you really?'

'Really.'

They are just preparing to leave – Mal is swinging round and he is puslnng her – when suddenly and without warning the roof creaks dully and the candle goes out.

'What has happened?'

'What?' he says. 'Nothing. Go on, Mal.'

'But I heard something.'

'I don't think you did. Please go on.'

'Is it safe?'

'Of course.'

A plank breaks. One end of it catches Vere a wicked blow on the head, the saturated earth of the mountain pours onto Mal's bent back, the sunlight streams through the rent in the roof, illuminating the wreckage.

Vere is suffering and in pain. He rubs his head with his hand and his eyes water. Mal, who cannot see the full extent of the catastrophe, calls to him.

Confused, frightened, not understanding what has happened yet determined to be equal to it, he answers calmly, 'There's nothing wrong, Mal. One of the planks, that's all. Can you get out?'

'But are you hurt?'

'No.'

She accepts his statement. He longs to tell her that he is

hurt, badly hurt, that the bump on his head is the size of a pigeon's egg; but he only asks her how she is managing. He wishes he were alone. He cannot face explanations, the thought of them makes his blood run cold. And there is Flora now: she is calling out: and Scamp is barking: and Nanny and Faith will be up by the willows.

He hears Flora say as Mal emerges from the house, 'Isn't it grand, Mademoiselle?' And then, 'Why Mademoiselle, you've mud all over your back!'

He hears Mal's worried answer, braces himself, then climbs over the broken doorstep into the sunlight.

Nanny appears beyond the water-pump with Faith in her arms.

'Where is it, Vere?' she calls.

'Hullo, Nanny.'

'Heavens, Mademoiselle, have you had a fall?'

Mal answers, 'Oh Nanny. No, we went into the house and part of it came down – it was an accident.'

'Oh dear,' Nanny says. 'Well, I'm sure the coat'll clean. So there's the house, Vere. It's fine! Mademoiselle, you let me have your coat afterwards, will you?'

And they converse together.

Flora, who has been looking at Vere and chewing her lower lip, asks where the house is damaged.

'All over,' he replies in an undertone.

'But no, you will mend it, Vere, it is not bad!' says Mal.

'Whatever's wrong with it you wouldn't know,' Nanny agrees. 'Well done, Vere.'

'And inside, Nanny,' Mal comforts him, 'it is wonderful! I love it!'

But the house is broken, he thinks. 'Let's go,' he says. 'Let's leave it.'

'You are not worried, are you, chéri?'

'No,' he replies.

'It is my fault?'

'No, Mal.'

'And you will put it right?'

'I don't know.'

Flora asks him if she can have a look. He says he does not care.

'Now Vere,' Nanny reproves from beyond the pump. 'What a way to speak to Flora. She's only trying to help. Show her what's the matter.'

He kicks at a stone while Flora and Mal stand by his house, discussing the damage. He notices that the roof is no higher than their waists. His enduring monument is a doll's house, clumsy, ramshackle, broken!

'Sweetheart,' Flora asks, 'it's just this plank, isn't it?'

'Could we not replace it now, Vere?'

'No,' he says. 'I'm afraid not, Mal. I'm afraid it's absolutely ruined actually.'

'But no!'

'Yes!' He laughs shortly.

'Oh Vere, I'll help you do it.'

'Will you, Flora? What about all these other things? This plank's pretty well bust too.' And he tugs viciously at the outside plank, the one with the heaviest sag. It does not move.

Nanny calls, 'What are you doing, Vere? You will bust it if you're not careful.'

'It is already,' he calls back angrily. That this weak plank should not even break at the correct moment enrages him.

'Don't, Vere,' says Mal.

'Look!' he cries. 'You see?'

The plank has cracked. Earth from the mountain cascades into the house.

'And this too!' he says, yanking at the corrugated-iron.

'Stop him, Flora,' Nanny calls.

'Sweetheart, Vere!'

The iron flops onto the ground, exposing the debris within.

'There!' he shouts. 'Do you see now? It's a rotten mess, that's all! I'm only showing you!'

He has never been so violent in his life. He scarcely knows what he is doing. A hard core of destructive furious misery sticks in his throat and chest.

Mal says, aghast, 'How could you, Vere?'

'Why not? Why shouldn't I? It's damn rotten anyway. All of it. Goodbye. I'm going.'

He flings away, but the excess of emotion makes his head throb and stars dance in front of his eyes. He stumbles over a wet sack.

'Vere!' Flora picks him up. 'What's the matter, Vere?'

'Nothing,' he sobs. 'I've hit my head. Goodbye!'

But he is not allowed to go. Flora feels the bump on his head and calls to Nanny. Mal feels the bump. Nanny takes him into the house. In the bathroom she applies lotions and reproaches him with having kept silent. This affords him some relief from his choking anger and despair. At least he has shown courage in the face of adversity. But he is ashamed of this sympathy won for the wrong reasons: he despises himself for welcoming it: and tearing himself from Nanny before she has completed her task he runs away down the nursery passage.

At the top of the stairs he meets Flora and Faith. Flora asks him where he is going. The gentleness of her question increases his anger. He answers bitingly, 'Out!' and deaf to her dismayed entreaties rushes down the stairs. On the bottom step he trips and turns his ankle. Sobbing with fury he hurls the side-door savagely open and hobbles onto the lawn.

'Vere!'

It is his mother. She is standing with his father outside the schoolroom french windows.

'You're not to open the door like that, Vere, you'll break the glass,' she says. 'Go back and shut it properly.'

He does as he is told and starts to cross the lawn.

'Vere! Say you're sorry to your mother,' his father calls.

'I'm sorry,' Vere shouts without pausing.

'Vere! Come here!' The boy stops. 'Come here.' But he does not move. He would rather die. 'Say you're sorry again.'

'I'm sorry, Mummy.'

'You mustn't bang doors like that, darling.'

Darling, he thinks – that empty word.

'You won't bang them any more, will you?'

He says nothing.

Uncomfortable, his mother calls across the lawn: 'Did you take Mal to see your house?'

He still says nothing.

His father mutters, 'Leave him alone.'

Yes, Vere thinks, leave me: I ask for nothing better.

'Would you like us to come and see your house, darling? We could now.'

'No,' he replies. 'It isn't ready. Thank you, Mummy.'

His father says, 'Come on,' and strolls off, whistling.

'Well – goodbye, darling,' his mother adds, smiling and waving her hand.

He turns away. At the mention of his house his heart has contracted. Even his parents' knowledge of it shocks him. But now his heart contracts at their lack of interest. He cannot comprehend his feelings.

He clambers onto the terrace wall and drops into the field of uncut hay. The fall jars him and hurts his ankle. He does not care. Water trickles down his legs inside his wellingtons as he limps through the wet hay. Clouds scurry and the sun warms – he does not notice: birds rise from beneath his feet – he does not start. On and on he walks without any sense of direction, conscious only of the turmoil within and the weight of his sorrow.

In a patch of purple clover he catches his foot and measures his length on the ground. He does not rise, he can bear no more. An endless aching sob is wrenched out of him, and another, and another. He has not the strength or the will to fight his sobs: they engulf him entirely. The tears course down his cheeks and mingle with the raindrops in the rich clover. He lies face downwards, clutching at grasses with his hands and resting his hot forehead on the soaked and soothing earth, and cries bitterly.

After a time his sobs lessen. There is an occasional catch in his throat and sometimes he shudders, but he feels drained, the causes of his misery recede, and he has to admit to himself that he is more hungry than anything else. He raises himself on an elbow and looks round.

He is not alone.

A startled hare is crouching only a few feet away, regarding him with flat and frightened eyes. He stares at the hare and the hare stares back. But this tawny animal, he thinks as he recovers from his surprise, is a fellow-creature, a friend; and he begins to rub his thumb and first finger together and to murmur softly, 'Come on. Come closer. Don't be afraid. Come on then, come on.'

The hare seems to hesitate. It lowers one ear a fraction of an inch and twitches its nose. Vere slides his hand along the ground, murmuring the while, but suddenly the hare is gone, bobbing unevenly, all legs and tucked-in tail, away into the hay.

Vere scrambles to his feet. The hare is nowhere to be seen, but under a tuft of grass beside the clover patch he finds a small smooth nest. Perhaps this is where he caught his foot: it is the hare's house and he has trodden on it. He kneels down, greatly distressed, places his hand in the oblong hollow and examines it from above and below. It is a perfect house, so snug and well-hidden, so natural. The hare must have been returning to it, full of pride and anticipation, only to find it crushed and overlaid by a fearsome stranger. What cruel fates, he thinks, await builders of houses. He tries to reshape the nest, but without success for the grasses are bruised and broken beyond repair.

He takes stock of his position. The tops of the grove trees are barely visible: he is miles from anywhere. After a last long look for the hare he sets out for home.

Whatever brought him so far into the field? Nanny and Flora must never know of his flight. No-one must know that he wept in the patch of clover, and no-one will know, except the hare. He and the hare are fellow-sufferers, he thinks. He wonders if the small animal is lying somewhere in the field, its eyes filled with tears, its brown body shaken with sobs, for like Vere the hare has lost its house. Their situation is the same. But no, he decides: the hare would accept its lot more philosophically. A hare's life probably consists of building houses and finding them destroyed. But then, he remembers sadly, so does my life . . .

The truth is, he thinks as he tramps through the hay, that one builds not for other people but for oneself: not really for praise or approval, but because one cannot do otherwise. Houses collapse, he thinks, are trodden on, are deserted when complete: but more houses are built, they always will be, he cannot imagine life without them.

His house is a failure. When he was building it – until a few hours back – he thought it beautiful. How can he have been so slapdash, so easily satisfied? He was going to have two rooms, a fire: he was going to sleep in it. What became of all his visions – that splendour, that magnificence? His broken house is a thing of the past. He will not visit it again. He is older now and not so hopeful, and the sweet and sanguine path that he has recently pursued is barred to him forever. One day, some day, he may build another house; but then he will build for the sake of building, modestly and in private. One day, perhaps . . . He cannot tell.

His resolution fortifies him, his spirits revive. The sun is shining blindingly after the rain. As a sign of fair weather the swallows mount and circle in the sky. Curiously, like some returning traveller, Vere observes afresh the gravel drying on the drive, the bare trunks of the beech trees, the grey extended house with white sash windows, the lawns, brick walls and climbing roses: and at sight of the dear unchanging scene, love that is remembered and new love unite in his heart, producing a tentative happiness, fragile yet pure and true.

It is five o'clock when he enters the nursery and tea is on the table. Flora greets him and helps him off with his wellingtons, but does not refer to the events of the afternoon. This raises a barrier between them, which Vere is considering how to broach when Nanny comes in with Faith and bluntly asks him where he has been.

'Out for a walk,' he says. 'I saw a hare.' Then he adds quickly, 'I'm sorry about earlier.'

Nanny accepts his apology as she straps Faith into her chair, asks after the bump on his head which he has forgotten, and says, sitting down, 'It was a shame about your house, Vere.'

'I know,' he says.

Flora sympathises and inquires if he will repair the damage.

'No,' he replies. 'I don't think I will, Flora.'

'You'll just have to build another house, Vere. That's what you'll have to do,' says Nanny.

'Yes,' he answers. And all of a sudden, to his utter amazement, he realises that he is once again in the grip of familiar excitement. The future, the radiant future with its smiling countenance, is holding out its hand, is claiming him again. He is already thinking where to build his house, his new house, a final and a faultless house, a house to end all houses. He cannot escape: he does not wish to. The frenzied yearnings of his soul, the singular joy, the labour and the pain – he embraces them like long-lost comrades. They are his destiny.

'Yes,' he says quietly to Nanny, 'I am going to.'

FOUR

LEO'S BIRTHDAY

'Nanny, how long before Leo comes back from school?'

'A week . . . Five days, three days, two days . . . Tomorrow, Vere.'

'Leo comes back tomorrow! And it's his birthday the day after, isn't it? Oh Nanny, what shall I give him?'

'Some little thing, Vere. Leo will have lots of presents.'

On the morning of the day of Leo's return Vere goes shopping in Long Cretton. Because of what Nanny has told him, wishing his present to be noticeably nice, he buys a flat chromium-plated knife for his brother, price five shillings and sixpence, which is more than he can afford. During the afternoon he uses it to carve his initials on the linoleum of the nursery passage, then he wraps it in tissue paper and puts it in his pocket, and with time to spare before leaving for the station, wanders into his brother's bedroom.

The figured bedspread is crisply white and unruffled, the windows are open, the tables bare, the drawers empty. Leo will live in this clean room, he thinks: Leo's things will litter the tables and overflow the drawers: this will be Leo's room. All will change here. All will alter in other ways. Private enterprises will be shelved: successes, failures, ideas, amusements will be divided, halved: the life with Leo, the happy active life, is again about to begin.

'Vere! Albert's waiting in the car.'

He runs downstairs. The house is neat and quiet, ready for

his parents, ready for Leo. He will laugh with Leo, tell and listen to stories; they will quarrel and fight. In a quarter of an hour Leo will be home. Vere is really looking forward to his arrival, to the excitement and disturbance.

'Are we late?' he asks anxiously, climbing into the car.

'Not unless the train's early,' answers Albert as he slides into his seat, closes the door, switches on the ignition, presses the self-starter, slips the car into gear and disengages the brake.

They move smoothly away.

'How do you do all those things so quickly?' Vere inquires.

'You ask your brother. He'll make a driver one of these days.'

'I'm going to learn to drive too,' says Vere.

After a pause Albert remarks, 'Well, you'll be getting up to some games now, I expect.'

'Why?'

'With that big brother of yours.'

'Oh, yes.'

'Give you someone to play with, won't it?'

'Yes, it will,' Vere agrees, starting to whistle.

'But you like playing on your ownsome, don't you?'

'Yes,' Vere replies.

On the station platform Mr Pick the station-master, red and green flags under his arm, greets Vere.

'Come to meet your brother, I expect?'

'That's right, Mr Pick.'

'He's the gentleman nowadays, isn't he, just like his father.'

'Yes.'

'Keep back from the line, sir, if you please.'

Although he buys a bar of slot-machine chocolate and weighs himself, Vere begins to wonder why he came to meet the train. Instead of wasting his time and money he thinks of a hundred interesting things he might be doing: and as for gaining a few extra moments of Leo's company – Leo will be home for weeks and months.

A bell clangs. Mr Pick unfurls his flags with a flourish and cries, 'London train, London train!' A hefty porter jumps onto the tracks, saunters across and heaves himself onto the platform.

'Where's the train?' asks Vere.

'Search me,' says the porter, winking at Albert.

A second bell clangs and a distant rumble is heard. Vere turns to the right, and here comes the train, streaming through the tunnel like a centipede, screaming and whistling, blasting out steam and smoke, tearing along!

'Back from the line, please!'

Now the train is close, slowing up, but it cannot stop – it will never stop in time! Mr Pick blows his whistle, waves his flags and his arms, knocks his gold-braided hat askew. The engine-driver, big and grimy, grins at Vere as he passes, taking no notice of Mr Pick's obscure signals. The brakes wheeze, the carriages jar. 'That'll do it, George,' calls the hefty porter. The train halts.

'Where are they, Albert, can you see them?'

A window is lowered and a round face pops out.

'Leo!' Vere rushes along the platform. 'Here they are, Albert! Leo, Leo!' He tugs at the heavy door. 'Hullo, Leo!'

'All right, don't shout,' says Leo, blushing. 'Hullo, Albert.'

'Good afternoon, Master Leo.'

'My trunk's in the van, Albert.'

'Right you are, Master Leo.'

Vere's mother steps down from the train. His father, inside the compartment, calls, 'Don't stand there, Vere, come and take my bag.'

'Help your father, darling,' his mother says.

'Go on, sloppy,' adds Leo, and the passengers in the compartment laugh.

Whistles blow: luggage is piled onto the platform: doors slam. The porter approaches.

'How many pieces, sir?'

'What?'

'Seven pieces, Dad, I counted them,' says Leo.

'Good boy. All right, come on. Don't lose my case, Vere.'

With a long-drawn sigh, a whistle and a puff, the train pulls out of the station.

Vere carries his father's attaché-case to the car. Leo is shaking hands with Mr Pick, who beams and touches his cap deferentially. Luggage is strapped onto the roof of the car and stowed in the boot. Albert mops his brow and orders Vere out of the way. Leo comes through the station gate.

'You sit in the front with Vere,' says his mother.

'Do I have to?'

'Oh Leo, don't be unkind. Vere's been longing to see you.'

'I don't mind,' Vere shrugs.

As they leave the station Mr Pick blows his whistle for the amusement of Leo, who laughs and waves, then the car swings away onto the main road.

How low Vere feels! If the holidays begin like this, how will they end? They last for years too. He wishes he had not spent so much money on the chromium-plated knife. He will have to keep it for himself, and give Leo as a birthday present the bar of railway chocolate. Why did he come to meet the train, what did he expect of his brother? He has never even cared for Leo. And Leo clearly does not care for him.

'Got me an expensive present for my birthday?'

'Yes,' Vere replies, taken by surprise.

'What is it?'

'I'm not going to tell you.'

'You are.'

'I'm not.'

'You lovely boy.'

'A jolly sight too expensive,' says Vere.

Leo pokes him in the ribs with his elbow and turns to talk to Albert.

Vere, winded by the blow, looks out of the window. He will certainly not give Leo the knife. He hates Leo. Never again will he be deceived by smiles and sudden questions. His brother is vile, horrible, whatever anyone else may think, rough, cruel and heartless: henceforth he will ignore him completely.

In spite of his firm resolve, at tea and during the triumphal tour of gardens, garages, stables and house, Vere continues to be tricked by flashing smiles and unexpected jokes into thinking he may be wrong in his estimate of his brother. Once or twice he even tries a joke and a smile himself. But his incautious hopes revive only to be crushed, and he grows sullen and wary, despises himself for being so lightly won, detests Leo, particularly for his assurance and fatal charm; while the pleasure that everyone appears to take in his brother's presence and jolly ways he does his utmost to discount.

Such is Vere's frame of mind at suppertime. He vows it will never change. However, when in the nursery Leo proposes that they should sleep in the same room, that they should straightaway move Vere's mattress and eat their soup and toast in bed, he finds himself not only listening with interest but actually agreeing; and a few moments later, as they struggle with the heap of bedding, he catches himself joining in Leo's infectious laughter; and when Leo says to him, 'Let's wash quickly, then we can play the wireless and have a chat,' he really wonders if he has not misjudged his brother.

Later still, snugly in bed, sipping cups of strong clear soup and munching dry toast, Leo observes, 'We might be in a theatre or a club, mightn't we, Jackson?'

'Yes,' Vere answers, once more taken unawares. This Jackson with whom the brothers sometimes identify themselves, the embodiment of all they consider grand and worldly, is a creation of their rare accord. For Leo to summon Jackson after the dissension of the afternoon is therefore curious. But pleased by what he accepts as a gesture of peace, Vere suggests, 'Have a cigar, Jackson,' and pulls a propelling pencil out of the pocket of his pyjamas.

'Light, please.'

'Coming up.'

He pretends to strike a match, Leo to puff and wave away smoke. They speak in deep voices, address each other as old boy, old man, old thing, etc., and offer each other loans of a thousand pounds.

'What are these cigars, Jackson?' asks Leo.

Vere gazes at him blankly, but remembering a phrase from *Settlers in Canada*, replies, 'They're some weeds I bought in Montreal.'

Leo giggles. 'Not bad at all,' he says. 'Waiter, more oysters for Mr Jackson. And I'll have another dozen or two. Thank you, waiter, keep the change.'

They dip their pieces of toast in their soup and with difficulty swallow mouthfuls whole. 'Good place, this,' they say. 'Nice to see you again.' Safely out of character they express their thoughts more freely.

'I say, Jackson, did you give the waiter a quid?' Vere inquires.

'I gave him a fiver, if you must know.'

They giggle. It seems so odd to say 'if you must know'. Leo calls for music and switches on the wireless. Vere conducts with serpentine movements of his long arms, tangling and untangling them. Leo laughs and sips his soup, and when Vere pretends that he cannot unwind his arms, cries with laughter and eventually dribbles.

Nanny comes and says goodnight. The light is turned off. Vere, lying on his mattress on the floor by Leo's bed, can just distinguish his brother's face above him, faintly picked out of the darkness by the glow of the wireless dial.

'Leo,' he says.

'Yes?'

'Happy birthday tomorrow.'

'Thanks. What's your present, Vere?'

'It's a chromium-plated knife, one of those really strong ones, Sheffield steel blades, you know.'

'Gosh, I've always wanted one like that.'

'Honestly, Leo?'

'Do you know what Mummy and Daddy are going to give me?'

'No,' says Vere.

'I asked for a bicycle or a gun.'

'Did you?'

'Yes.'

'Golly,' Vere bursts out, 'if they've given you a gun, Leo! I'd rather have a gun than anything in the world.'

'You can use mine.'

'Thanks awfully!'

Leo says, 'I'd rather have a bicycle. Do you swear you don't know?'

'Yes, I swear.'

'What shall we do tomorrow?'

'Let's go shooting.'

'Has Mrs Lark made me a cake?'

'I think so. I know, let's cook our lunch out of doors.'

'They'd never let us.'

'Yes, they would. It is your birthday.'

'Gosh, I'm sleepy.'

'Don't go to sleep yet, Leo.' A pause. 'Leo, let's make tomorrow specially nice.'

'All right.'

'Do you think it will be a gun?'

'I hope it's a bicycle.'

'Leo . . . Thanks for saying I can shoot with it.'

'That's all right.'

'Well . . . Goodnight, Leo.'

'Goodnight, Vere.'

The wireless is switched off and the room is in total darkness. Leo tosses once in his bed, then begins to breathe regularly. A suggestion of light, blue-green like the depths of the sea, tinges the still curtains. Vere lies awake on his hard mattress.

Leo is his best friend, there is no escaping the fact. Leo is the most decent, the kindest, funniest – the closest friend he has. He could not have been more generous about the gun: perhaps he will give Vere a share of it: and how he enjoys a joke, how he laughs! He can be nice when he tries, that is the truth about Leo: and when he does not try, then he is nasty. He ought not to have called Vere 'sloppy' on the station platform. For that matter he ought not to have behaved in such a careless and high-handed way. But, Vere wonders, is he in any position to complain? Of his own free will he is lying on the floor while Leo comfortably reclines in bed; without persuasion he spoke of the knife; and he said goodnight, although he wanted to go on talking, because Leo decided he was sleepy. It is strange, Vere thinks, that he should permit Leo to twist him round his little finger, strange and discreditable. For Leo has behaved badly – that blow in the car was outrageous. No; his brother's conduct does not stand examination, and it is weak to be taken in, deceived by random smiles and sweet words, when Leo has proved himself times without number brutal and unloving.

He turns over in bed and closes his eyes. In future he will be more careful. He will not commit himself so readily or to the same extent. He will question and weigh, and with steady judgment control their relations. Feeling that he has freed himself from Leo's subtle spell, feeling once again thoroughly Vere, with a final happy twinge of anticipation at the prospect of the following day, he goes peacefully to sleep.

The next morning the brothers wake at seven-thirty. Vere wishes Leo a happy birthday and gives him the knife. Leo thanks him warmly and lays it on his bedside table. For an hour they fight, struggle, laugh and tumble about on the beds. At eight-thirty their father, in pyjamas and down-at-heel slippers, a shaving-brush in his hand, a heavy lather on his chin, comes to bid them good morning. But neither he nor the boys can think of anything to say to each other, and after he has left, Leo and Vere dress and go to breakfast in the nursery. Nanny, Flora, Faith, and Mary and Karen, the older girls, enter and give Leo their presents. From Nanny he receives four marked handkerchiefs, from Flora a box of peppermint creams, from Mary a book about a boys' school, from Karen another box of peppermint creams, and from Faith a jersey which Nanny has been knitting for the last two weeks. He accepts the gifts gracefully, with exclamations and kisses, leaves them on the floor and takes his place at the table.

As soon as grace has been said Vere puts forward his plan for the picnic. Mary and Karen are full of enthusiasm, which Leo now reflects. They plead with Nanny: provided they can obtain their mother's consent she at length agrees to help them. Cries of glee break out on all sides. Where will they have the picnic? Faith batters her plate with her spoon. Who will they ask? What will they eat and how will they cook it? Who will cook it? Will it be fine, will they obtain permission?

Breakfast is finished and the children, flushed, bright-eyed, eagerly chattering, approach the solemn door at the top of the front stairs. They try to decide who shall knock on the door, giggle, hush one another, giggle louder and push Leo forward. He scratches at the panel with his fingernails.

'Come in.'

The children enter their mother's room. She is lying in bed, pale and composed, eating her breakfast of a boiled egg and white bread-and-butter with the crusts removed.

'Good morning, darlings,' she says.

'Good morning, Mummy,' they answer, as in turn they lean across and kiss her.

'Happy birthday, Leo darling.'

'Thank you, Mummy.'

'Your present is downstairs. Will you wait to see it till I get up, or would you like to go now?'

Leo, who in the general excitement has forgotten about his birthday, tactfully agrees to wait.

'It's from Daddy and me,' his mother says. 'I hope you'll like it.'

Leo replies, 'I bet I will,' and glances at the others. 'Mummy,' he starts, pauses, then inquires, 'Don't you like toast with your egg, Mummy?'

But Mary interrupts in a commanding voice, 'Leo!'

'What's the matter, darling?'

'Go on, Leo,' orders Mary.

'What is it, Leo?' asks his mother.

'Well, we were wondering, Mummy, actually, if you'd let us have a picnic, as a sort of birthday treat? Nanny says she doesn't mind and we would love it. Could we?'

'But tea is all arranged indoors.'

'No no – for lunch!' chime in the others. 'We want to cook our lunch. Oh Mummy, please!'

'As a special treat,' repeats Leo appealingly.

'Yes, I think you could, if you really want to.'

The children, who have been standing in tense postures round the room, look at each other, draw deep breaths and thank their mother. Smiles spread across their faces and they troop modestly through the door which Leo, after making an arrangement to meet his mother in half an hour, discreetly closes. The door-handle clicks: they tear along the passage and hustle helter-skelter into the nursery. They shout the glad news at the tops of their voices, leap about, congratulate Leo and pat him on the back as hard as they can. Laughing and arguing they mill round Nanny and Flora, planning the picnic. They will roast a chicken on a spit: no, they will fry eggs, bacon and sausages: no, they will bake potatoes in the bonfire: no, they will – shall – must have mashed potato. And what pudding, heavens above, what pudding? Banana fritters, treacle tart? And where will they have their picnic, where, where?

'Mary and Karen,' Nanny says at last, 'you go to Mrs Lark and ask her nicely, nicely mind, what she'll let you have. Flora, run after the girls and see they don't get into trouble. And Leo, you go with Vere and say good morning to Mademoiselle and ask her if she'd care to join us. And we'll meet back here. Off you go now.'

The boys caper down the passage, find Mal and invite her to the picnic. She accepts with pleasure and gives Leo his present, a tie with a design of Sealyhams' heads. Leaving her they go to the smoking-room, where they meet their father.

'Is Mummy down?' asks Leo.

Vere tells his father about the picnic.

'Are they going to roast you and eat you for dinner?'

'Oh Dad!'

Leo has run out of the room and now returns arm-in-arm with his mother. She loves these little attentions and is smiling happily.

'Shall we let him have his present?' she asks, laying her hand on Leo's head.

They form into a procession, pass through the study, go out by the back-door, cross the yard and enter the hot and musty brushing-room. On the deal table, stained and shiny with boot-polish, is a long canvas gun-case.

'It's a gun,' says Vere from the doorway. The sight of the case, bulging and reinforced with strongly sewn leather, so new, clean and manly, makes him shiver with delight.

'A gun! Oh Mummy, Dad, that's marvellous,' says Leo, kissing his parents. 'I wanted one more than anything. Thank you so much!'

His father, with red and slightly shaking fingers, begins to unbuckle the end. 'You go very carefully with this now, Leo. Stand clear,' he says, sliding the gun out of the cover.

Vere says, 'It can't be loaded.'

'You be quiet and do as I tell you.'

'Yes, you be quiet,' adds Leo.

But Vere is too intent on the wonderful object which his father gingerly handles even to laugh. He has eyes for nothing but the gun, a small shotgun, exquisitely made, reminiscent of a hundred beloved passages from *Settlers in Canada*. His father opens and closes the breech, looks down the barrel, raises the gun to his shoulder once or twice, then holds it out to Leo. Vere leans over his brother's shoulder. The gun's stock is of walnut, intricately whorled; the breech and trigger-guard are chased and figured; the blued steel of the barrel is dark and thinly oiled; the foresight is brassy and bright.

'Do you like it, darling?'

Leo, copying his father's actions, answers, 'I certainly do!'

'Can I hold it?' asks Vere.

'Don't go and drop it.'

'Of course I won't.'

He takes the gun and opens the breech. Its mechanism is as fine and precise as a watch. Pointing the barrel towards the light he stares through it. The silver barrelling is perfect. The winding rings, which give direction to the shot, glint and gleam with trapped brightness. He closes the gun gently and traces with his finger the circular markings on the smooth stock.

The others are talking. 'Can we let it off?' he interrupts.

'What, in here?' jokes Leo.

'You must take the boys out shooting, David.'

'Oh yes, this evening – after tea, Dad!'

'Perhaps you could shoot a pigeon, just to show them, David.'

'It's the wrong time of year.'

'Oh please, Dad!'

Leo begs his father, Vere beseeches him. Eventually he consents. The boys must behave, do as they are bid, sit very still and quiet. They agree to everything. In that case, as long as it does not rain, he will take them shooting.

The gun is replaced in its cover and stood in the gun-rack. Leo once again thanks his parents and the brothers return to the nursery.

Preparations for the picnic are proceeding apace. Chops, tomatoes, carrots and potatoes have been wheedled out of Mrs Lark, also a frying-pan and a kettle. Packages in grease-proof paper, baskets, rugs, newspaper and sticks are scattered over the nursery table.

'What about our pudding?' question the boys.

'Oh, didn't we tell you? Ice-cream,' answer the girls with sly smiles.

Nanny enters the nursery and issues orders like a general. 'Now, have you salt and pepper?'

'Salt and pepper, Vere,' says Flora, pointing to the dresser.

'And milk?'

'Mary, ask Mrs Lark for milk, we forgot that,' says Flora.

'And now, where shall we have our picnic?'

Mary suggests the farm, Karen the wood, Leo a field or down the drive.

Nanny says, 'Flora, you take these things when you're ready, and you and the children choose the place. Not too far away, and let's have some water close, and sticks for the fire. And I'll come soon with Faith and find you.'

Everyone hurries to obey Nanny's commands. The table is piled higher and higher with stores and equipment. Flora stands beside it, saying to herself, 'Oh dash, the orangeade . . . Oh dash, the ice-cream wafers!' As each omission occurs to her she clicks her tongue and tosses her head, and once, when Vere points out that they have forgotten a box of matches, she laughs through her teeth and buries her face in her hands. But finally all is complete. The children, reassembled in the nursery, load one another like pack animals and shout instructions over their shoulders. Karen leads the caravan down the passage and out of the house; Mary and Leo follow; Flora, with Vere trotting beside her, brings up the rear.

It is a day of sun, cloud and wind. The shadows of the trees seem to be blown across the gravel and short grass of the drive. Jackdaws wheel and plummet round the hollow elm, cavort in the swift currents of the air, uttering cracked and piercing notes, settle on swaying twigs and soar again into the sky.

The spot that Flora chooses for the picnic is a mossy bank under the nut-hedge at the end of the garden. The children gratefully deposit their loads, and Leo and Vere are despatched to gather wood for the bonfire. It is lit by the time they return and Karen is blowing it up, her nose an inch from the undecided flame. The wind changes. She emerges from smoke and fire with singed eyebrows and a cry of despair that turns into laughter. What does it matter? Nothing matters today. Everything is funny, everything amuses. The children settle to their tasks. Flora lifts the lid of the ice-cream machine and allows them a taste. They reach into the freezing container, packed round with chips of broken ice, and scrape the dripping whisk with their fingers.

Nanny arrives. Fat begins to bubble and spit in the frying-pan, blue smoke to rise. Flora and Mary prod at the white potato slices with palette-knives; Leo lies on his stomach, tending a pile of ashes that he calls the oven; Vere fetches and carries, filling the kettle, supplying Karen with fuel. Returning from one of his errands he finds his father, leaning with crossed arms on a tall thumb-stick, watching the others.

'Hullo, you little rat.'

'Hullo, Dad.'

'Doesn't it smell good?' His father sniffs.

'Stay and have lunch,' says Vere.

'No, old boy.'

'Please do.'

'There won't be much left by the time you've finished, will there?' His eyes crinkle. 'I've got my lunch indoors.' And scarcely noticed by the picnickers he strolls away.

Sensing of a sudden his father's exclusion, his loneliness, and recalling his early morning visit – the way he smiled through his shaving-soap, not knowing what to say – Vere feels unexpectedly sad, sorry that he cannot share with his father the wonder of this day, glad that at least he asked him to stay. Later, he thinks as he watches the broad retreating figure, we will go shooting together.

The brisk wind hustles the clouds across the sky, and this cloud, which for a second masks Vere's sun, passes like those above. Warmth and light are everywhere again, movement is general. 'Vere, more sticks. Wash this pan, Vere.' He steps with perilous agility between the crouched and concentrated figures, smoke in his eyes, smuts in his hair, laughter never far from his lips. The tempo of activity increases. He receives a blow on the leg from Leo – 'Get your great foot out of the chips' – upsets water over Mary, but he only laughs, amused even by his repeated apologies. 'Sorry, look out, sorry, sorry . . .' He hugs Flora – she is working so hard – lifts her linen hat and kisses the top of her head. 'Sweetheart,' she cries. 'Sorry, Flora.' When he replaces her hat the shadow of the soft white brim unevenly divides her smiling face. 'Oh Flora, sorry,' he says.

His mother and Mal approach. 'How are you getting on?'

'You don't know what fun we're having, Mummy!'

'Come and look in my oven,' calls Leo. 'My eyebrows are burnt off,' Karen says. Vere has never seen his mother so lively. He leads her round by the hand, pointing out this and that, offering her a chip, a carrot, while Mal crows her appreciation in broken English. 'Stay, Mummy, you and Daddy stay.'

'No, darling, we'll be out afterwards. Have a lovely lunch.'

'We will!'

'Goodbye, darlings.'

'Goodbye, Mummy.' A rug is spread on the bank and Mal lowers herself onto it with groans and laughter. Flora says, 'I think we're ready.'

The children circle the fire with burning faces, eyes fixed on Nanny and Flora, mouths watering. Crumbling fried potatoes are ladled onto the plates they hold out, burnt carrots and tomatoes, sizzling chops. They mutter in indistinct voices at the least injustice, wishing their helpings could be weighed on a pair of scales. Hunks of crisp bread are cut, knives and forks distributed. Grace is said. They sit, and in hushed and reverent silence gulp down the first unforgettable mouthfuls.

But every mouthful of that luncheon under the nut-hedge is unforgettable. As it begins so it continues. The chops are different from any Vere has tasted: everything is different: ice-cream was never, never like this.

Satisfied, replete, partly sheltered from the wind which rustles and shakes the branches of the hazel-trees and causes the embers of the fire to glow intermittently, the children loll on the bank in easy attitudes. The filtered sunlight flecks the rich mosses: they lie on their backs and touch them with their outstretched hands. Wouldn't it be nice, they ask each other lazily, to have a carpet of moss? It would be soft, springy, and the merging shades of green, the specks of gold and purest white – why, they would provide variety and contrast. Wouldn't it be nice, they murmur, to live always in this pleasant mottling sunlight, under the busy but reflective sky? To eat as they have eaten, to work as they have worked, to relax as they are relaxing – what a life that would be! Their thoughts, indolently voiced, play upon their separate imaginations, summon for each an individual heaven. Freely their fancies roam, distinct, personal – perhaps never to be shared. Yet as they dream, stroking the mosses, sinking their fingers to feel the deep hoarded moisture of the earth, the magic of this moment under the nut-hedge – the sunlight, the rapt peacefulness of the hour, the quiet conversation of the grown-ups, the fall of the fire – permeates their private worlds and unites in a way and for a brief instant the inexpressible longings of their ardent and tender hearts.

Somebody stirs. The moment is gone. But the children, after they have cleared the picnic and taken it indoors, return to the garden and lie on the mown grass. They stare at the sky, fling out their arms, as if they believe that by imitating their previous postures they will succeed in recapturing their previous mood. They discover that the moment is truly gone, truly lost. They wish to speak of it but do not know what words to use, how to express themselves. They enthuse over the picnic and pause; their lips part in secret smiles; their eyes are eloquent, lingering; they are silent. They feel that under the nut-hedge they experienced a closeness to each other and to all things that was unique and wonderful: but as their talk is forced into other channels their minds jib, doubt, shy away from the strangeness of their fleeting illumination. They speak of what is safe, understood. A desire to re-establish themselves in the characters by which they are recognised, and out of which they seem to have slipped, possesses them. They fear they have given themselves away, allowed strangers to trespass on the intimate preserves that they will one day, one day throw open, but not yet, not now, not like this: and a sense of discovery, of being found out, causes them embarrassment. So they turn from the memory of the moment on the mossy bank, the joy of that unspoken union, and grapple once more with the world they know, the world of other people, sure and familiar, normal, certain, right.

The wind dies down. The children roll into the shade of an apple-tree.

'Isn't it hot?' they say.

'It must be the hottest day of the year.'

They take off their shoes and socks and race each other to the lilypool. Dangling their legs in the cool water, dancing about on the hot paving-stones, applying their thumbs to the nozzle of the fountain, they pass the afternoon. When Nanny leans out of the nursery window to ring the bell for tea she sees four figures, two wearing only trousers turned up to the knees and two in clinging vests and blue knickers, darting with damp abandon round the pool. She rings the bell imperiously.

Astonished by the state in which they find themselves, the children collect their discarded clothes and straggle indoors. After washing and changing they go down to the dining-room and eat a large tea. As soon as the meal is finished Vere reminds his father of his promise.

'What promise?'

'To take us shooting, Dad.'

His father, who has been sitting silently at the head of the table, puts out his arm and catches the boy round the waist. 'You want to go, don't you?' he says, smiling indulgently and squeezing Vere's chin with the finger and thumb of his free hand. 'Don't you, little monkey?'

'Yes, Dad. Please, you will take us?'

'All right then, later,' he agrees.

It is past the brothers' usual bed-time when they meet their father in the brushing-room. He has put on a rough tweed coat and a cap, and carries a shooting-stick and a box of cartridges. They take the gun out of the rack and Leo is shown how to hold it in the crook of his arm: Vere is entrusted with the cartridges and they sally forth.

The wind has dropped completely. High gauzy cloud is drawn across the sky and the spreading scene is rosily sunlit. Midges swarm under the trees, early moths flutter from tufts of grass.

'Dad,' says Vere, running to keep up, 'one evening with Mr Ball' – Mr Ball is the farmer – 'I went shooting, and we walked for miles. And on the other side of the wood a really high pigeon came over and he shot it dead. It fell round and round, with its wings out, round and round – it took ages to come down. Do pigeons always fall like that?'

'Not always, no.'

'Another time Mr Ball shot a pigeon, but that was with a rifle, sitting. It was frightfully difficult though, up in a big tree, and he got it through the heart. That one fell with a thump.'

Leo says, 'Shut up, Vere, you'll scare everything off.'

'Have you shot many pigeons, Dad?' Vere asks in a loud whisper.

'In my time I have.'

'Will we get one this evening?'

'We might.'

'Are you going to shoot flying?'

'That's the idea.'

They enter the wood. The boys follow their father down a rutted overgrown track. Amongst some dark fir-trees they stop.

'This ought to do it.'

'Here, Dad?'

'Yes. Now; I'll shoot through that opening.' He points up. 'Give me the gun, Leo. Vere, empty those cartridges into my pocket.'

'All of them, Dad?'

'Yes. Go and sit over there now, and listen, don't talk or move. Do you understand?'

'Yes, Dad.'

The brothers choose trees about ten yards from their father, sit with their backs against the trunks and clasp their drawn-up knees with their arms. The drooping branches cast a deep shade on the earth which is yellow-brown and strewn with pine-needles. Here and there shafts of light arrow down and fasten brilliantly on a skeleton branch or a fir-cone gnawed by squirrels. Motes whirl profusely in the sunbeams, the air is musky and resinous, a humming silence prevails in which the least sound echoes and multiplies.

A metallic click. Vere starts. His father, sitting on his shooting-stick beneath the patch of sky – blue between the fir-trees – has opened the gun. He slips a cartridge into the breech. Another click as he closes it and again Vere starts. His father reaches for a cigarette and strikes a match. It rasps harshly against the side of the box, flares for a second and is flicked aside. Tobacco smoke drifts in the clearing, heavy, blue, aromatic. His father begins to whistle softly, looking at his shoes, his back rounded.

Leo leans across and plucks Vere's sleeve. 'Which way will the pigeons come?' he whispers.

'I don't know.'

'It's exciting, isn't it?'

Vere nods. His father swivels on his stick, smiling. A jay scolds in a nearby tree. Suddenly there is a rushing flutter of wings as the first pigeon glides overhead and then veers widely away.

Leo calls out. His father stands up, throws his cigarette onto the pine-needles, grips the gun with both hands. Smoke from the cigarette clings to the ground. A second pigeon sweeps in, a third, a fourth. 'Why doesn't he shoot?' asks Leo, and Vere answers, 'They're all too far.' The boys gaze upwards, straining their eyes, the bark of the trees rough against their shoulders. A fly buzzes discordantly and settles on Vere's forehead.

'Dad,' warns Leo.

A fifth pigeon is sweeping in. Vere sees it and looks at his father. He is tense now, feet apart, gun slightly raised. The pigeon sails over the treetops. There is a loud bang and it swerves out of sight.

'Did you get it, Dad?' cries Leo.

'No.'

'Are you sure, Dad?'

His father reloads the gun without answering. More pigeons fly over the clearing. Vere picks up an empty brass-tipped cartridge and sniffs it. Thicker and thicker fly the pigeons, again and again the gun bangs. In the dimming light Vere can discern the taut expression on his father's face, and as he continues to miss the looming birds, can hear him cursing under his breath. He wishes he could tell his father how happy he is, or could be, sniffing the acrid cartridge, sitting in the shady wood: he wishes his father would not repeat, 'I can't shoot with this damn gun,' would smile or whistle or make a quacking noise. But Vere understands that his father cannot do any of these things because he is too fine, too splendid: that if he could laugh when he missed a pigeon, if he could eat ice-cream under the nut-hedge, then he would be different – a friend: and recalling his affectionate gesture at the tea-table, his wistful question 'Don't you, little monkey?' and his sad flattered smile, the boy senses for the second time that loneliness which touched him before the picnic and which he longs to be able to disperse.

It is evening now. A scarlet flash is visible when the gun is fired. The patch of sky takes on a sunset colour and under the fir-trees all is dusky, indistinct.

'Leo.'

'Dad?'

'Give me some more cartridges.'

'Have you got any more?' Leo asks Vere.

'No.'

'We haven't any more, Dad.'

There is a pause. Vere says carefully, 'Can you see to shoot, Dad?'

'I can see all right. There's something wrong with the gun, I don't know!'

'But it's fun, Dad, being here.'

His father remarks irritably, 'I've never known anything like these midges!'

Vere can think of no answer. In the unsettled silence he hears Leo sharply scratch his ankle, his father's foot scrape against the shooting-stick. The day is not what it was, none of it is the same. He begins to feel tired. He would like to go home.

Suddenly the gun explodes. There is a whirling overhead, then a curious thud. Leo is on his feet and his father is saying, 'I think I got that one – did I get it, Leo? Go and look to the left – I think I got it!' And his voice is changed.

Vere jumps up. Somewhere a branch cracks, another shivers. Something is falling to the ground – wings flap loudly once. 'Where is it?' calls Leo. They hunt under the fir-trees. 'Here, Leo, Vere, here we are!' The boys run – bent double – beneath the spiky branches. Their father is standing by the dead pigeon which lies with its head unnaturally twisted to one side. 'Well done, Dad,' they say. 'Good shot, well done! Oh Dad, well done!' Some feathers, pale, luminous, sway softly downwards and light on the dark earth.

'That was the last cartridge,' their father is saying in his excited voice. 'I was just going to give up. I couldn't see a damn thing. Then this chap comes over! Here you are, old boy, here's your gun. There's not much wrong with it if you shoot straight.' He laughs, feeling for a cigarette, and the boys laugh too. 'You take the pigeon, Vere. God knows what time it is. Come on.'

He goes to fetch his shooting-stick. Vere picks up the warm pigeon and follows Leo onto the track.

'It must be frightfully late.'

'Yes,' Vere murmurs.

'Gosh, I enjoyed that.'

'So did I.'

'Is the pigeon heavy?'

'Yes, Leo, quite.'

A cigarette glows and their father approaches out of the gloom.

'Come on, rabbits, time to go home.'

They file along the path, Vere stroking the pigeon and smoothing its ruffled downy feathers, and climb the gate into the field. A corn-coloured moon, round and low, rises already over the nestling farm. The grass beneath their feet is dim and dewy. Leo puts his arm through Vere's.

'Gosh, it's nice to be back.'

'Oh Leo, I wish it was always like this, always your birthday.'

'It's only the first day of the holidays.'

'It has been specially nice, hasn't it?'

'Yes.'

'Leo, I'm glad you're back.'

Their father waits for them. They run to catch up and walk on either side of him with stretching legs.

'Is the pigeon safe?'

'Yes, Dad.'

'Don't let it fly away.'

'I'm holding it in my arms.'

A snatch of tuneless whistle.

'Well, we got one after all.'

'Yes.'

'Did you think we wouldn't?'

'Well . . . For a bit.'

The boys look up at their father, smiling. He tosses his cigarette aside and rests his hands on their shoulders.

'Are you happy now?'

'Yes, Dad.'

'Are you, Dad?'

'You monkey . . . Yes, I am.'

They stumble over the uneven turf and bump against each other, as with full hearts they fix their eyes on the bright windows of the house.

1939

FIVE

WINTER

Leo's holidays pass. The sixty-five days succeed one another, some sweet, some sad, some light, some dark – none like Leo's birthday.

Walking home from the wood that evening Vere's happiness seemed complete. He did not think – he was too happy – but he savoured his feelings of joy and fellowship, and as he bumped against his father in the twilit field, fully and without reserve he welcomed his emotions, believing he had won them for himself and they were his forever.

Vere's happiness does not last. The morning after Leo's birthday his father says to him, 'Don't you try to get me to take you shooting again, you monkey. Your mother says you're looking tired.'

These words confuse the boy. He does not know what to do or to say. The gap between him and his father, over which their hands had touched so warmly, so hopefully, widens and becomes impassable. 'Does she, Dad?' he replies eventually, raising his voice as if to make himself heard across the empty spaces.

The children never again approach the moment of union they knew under the nut-hedge. Rifts open between them as the holidays progress, squabbles break out. Leo becomes friendly with an older boy from his school. Once he has to be persuaded to allow Vere to join in their swaggering enterprises. After that the brothers go their separate ways, Leo laughingly with his friend, Vere distractedly, alone, unsettled. But the holidays end and Leo returns to school. Two days after his departure Vere finds the chromium-plated knife in the drawer of the bedside table. It is still wrapped in tissue-paper and there is a spot of rust on one of the Sheffield steel blades. He turns the knife over in his hand, tries its sharpness on the ball of his thumb, pockets it and does not go again into Leo's room.

Autumn comes and leaves are blown at night against the shuttered windows. Extra blankets are put on the beds and Albert comes in one morning to see to the radiators. Bonfires smoulder down the drive, flaring and dying out, and the gardeners pause in their work to blow on their red, chapped hands.

'When is autumn winter, Nanny?'

'It's winter now, child, winter now.'

Long cosy evenings are spent round the nursery fire. Loving without fear and certain of love, Vere regains his poise and concentration. Books are read, *The Last of the Mohicans, Children of the New Forest.* He gazes into the embers, bemused, contented, while Flora reads in her soft voice, looking up as she turns a page, and Nanny's knitting-needles click. His parents are seldom at home. They come and go, in dark London clothes, in tailored tweeds, in hunting clothes, changed for dinner: gentle, undemanding, they move like shadows through these quiet weeks. October passes, November . . . The dashing exploits of the summer months seem far away. He is in tune with winter now, its stoic calm, its peace, its peculiar clinging sadness.

December . . . The windows of the shops in Long Cretton are tricked out with tinsel. 'Christmas is coming, the geese are getting fat . . .'

'Go on, sweetheart.'

'Please put a penny . . .'

'Go on.'

'In the young boy's hat!' How lovely to make Flora laugh. 'Flora, we never kept our ducks, did we?'

'We'll buy some after Christmas, sweetheart, and fatten them up and make a nice bit of money.'

'Really, Flora?'

'Honestly.' But Christmas is coming and V[illegible] money now.

Mrs Lark calls him into the kitchen one evening [illegible] Christmas pudding. 'Put the money in, my dear, an[illegible] up,' she says, pointing to a pile of sixpences and thre[illegible]ny bits that stand by the big brown bowl. While Vere drops the coins one by one into the heavy mixture and wields the wooden spoon with both hands, Mrs Lark leans on the kitchen table – her arm bent sharply outwards at the elbow – and regards him with her brooding black eyes. Suddenly she says, 'We're off to a dance on Christmas night.'

'Can you dance, Mrs Lark?' asks Vere.

'Dance?' Her eyes flash. 'I was born dancing! Ethel,' she shouts to the scullery-maid, a stolid country girl supposed to be wrong in the head. 'Ethel, can I dance?'

'You can, Mrs Lark,' says Ethel.

'Mister Vere and me's going dancing Christmas night.'

'Oh fancy,' Ethel giggles.

'Now then, none of that,' snaps Mrs Lark, still without a smile, and turns to Vere. 'Made your wish, my dear?'

He closes his eyes, and unable to think of anything better, wishes for a happy Christmas.

'Right-ho,' says Mrs Lark. 'Here's hoping your wish comes true and thanks for the kind assistance. And remember, Christmas night!'

This conversation with Mrs Lark excites Vere unexpectedly. He begins to take a more active interest in the preparations that are stealthily going forward around him: he helps to deck the nursery with streamers and silver stars, and, the day before Leo returns, with dark green holly: he wakes early with twinges of anticipation and counts the busy cheerful days. But he cannot throw off that peculiar sadness – that sadness of the season – a regret for what is past, a reaching-out for what he does not know, a wistful hope, an unexplained despair, which makes him pause in the act of balancing a sprig of holly on a picture and gaze into Flora's eyes, or at Nanny drying Faith's clothes in front of the fire, as if for the last time.

On the afternoon of the day before Christmas the children

wrap their presents. Vere's are already wrapped and put away, and he sits on the nursery sofa, watching, smiling, strangely untouched by the merry bustle and noise. From time to time he wanders between the intent figures, tries to tease Leo who tells him to go away, strokes Karen's hair and receives a cold look, and imagines that if only somebody would laugh at his jokes his depression would instantly vanish. After tea on the same day the children go carol-singing. Muffled in their warmest clothes they arrive at Albert's cottage, open their hymn-books with clumsy gloved hands, fumble with torches and raise their treble voices in uncertain unison. 'Silent night, holy night . . .' Leo leads them, and his clear notes, the simple carol, the crisp mysterious night which obliterates familiar landmarks, produce little by little a sense of wonder and release in Vere's heart. It is Christmas Eve, he tells himself, the bright stars are shining; nothing is the matter, nothing is wrong.

But that evening as he lies in his narrow bed Vere's sadness returns. And the next day – Christmas day – it is no better. As soon as tea is finished he slips out of the dining-room, where Faith is crying for the fourth time and Leo is performing card-tricks on the floor, and rests his head against the wall of the dark passage. Bella, emerging from the pantry, sees him and asks why he is not with the others. He replies that he does not know.

The character of his sadness has definitely changed. It is no longer peculiar, but actual – even dangerous. Bella invites him into the servants' hall. He follows her and begins to eat sweet chestnuts which Ethel is roasting in the fire. The room is hot and bright, and Ethel laughs at everything he says. Mrs Lark comes in, dressed for the dance. Her black locks are oiled and curled, her black eyes glint and dart, she seems to be covered in black beads, and her powdered flesh looks luminous. He tries to excuse himself, but she seizes him by the hand and leads him into the kitchen. He is dancing with Mrs Lark round the kitchen table, round and round, pretending to join in resounding laughter. Light is reflected from copper pots, staring faces fill the doorway. He bumps into the cook – she is like a cushion, feels her soft arms about him, hears her fruity voice, is stifled by her scent. His head is whirling. Flora calls. He goes upstairs.

That night, when all is quiet, Vere wakes and is sick. His illness has begun. He surrenders to it with relief as he could not surrender to his incomprehensible sadness. He is sick throughout the remainder of the night and in the morning feels pale and wasted. His mother appears – he is sick: his father, Dr Gail – he is sick. The day passes, the night – the night again, the day. He loses count of time.

'I'm ill, Flora.'

'Yes, sweetheart.'

'I've been ill for ages.'

'Don't talk. Try and sleep.'

'When was Christmas?'

'Three days ago.'

'Oh Flora.'

'Yes, sweetheart, I'm here, I'm here.'

He is often frightened. His coughing and his sickness frighten him. Only Nanny's hand, or Flora's – only their ready hands, for which he reaches at all hours of the day and night, still his fear. He sleeps, waking to the smell of enamel bowls and clean linen, sleeps again and dreams. One dream terrifies him. He is being forced to swallow huge moving furry shapes: they balloon out as they approach him, dark and living: he swallows and swallows, but cannot swallow quick enough: they slide over his head like sticky sacks: he becomes a shape himself and is carried away. He has other dreams. Sometimes he is kissing his father, hugging and kissing him, speaking of his love and admiration, and his father is smiling fondly and laying his shaky hand on Vere's refreshed forehead. Or he is in the garden, pushing his way through one of the yew hedges: he sees his mother in the distance, gathering flowers, beside blossomy trees full of singing birds, under a blue sky: he wrestles through the hedge into the sunlit garden, and suddenly he is unbelievably happy, so happy that he wants to cry.

'What's the matter with me, Flora?'

'You've got whooping-cough, Vere.'

Detached incidents, like phrases of music, stick in his mind:

shooting the pigeon on Leo's birthday, the chromium-plated knife, the hare's nest in the field of clover, the ride on Mr White's motorbicycle. But the grinding rotation of his thoughts mills these recollections into a dust.

He is very ill. He knows this for certain when a nurse arrives. Stretching out his hand to Nanny or Flora and touching instead the nurse's starched apron, he cries. One evening he sits up in bed and says he is hungry. The nurse recommends calves-foot jelly, but Vere, with tears in his eyes, begs Nanny for oranges.

'Yes, Vere, in a minute, I'll prepare them.'

Nanny brings him the oranges. She has peeled and sliced them beautifully, removed all pips and skin, and sprinkled them with sugar. He eats voraciously, his mouth watering.

'Oh Nanny, how good they are!'

'I'm glad to see you eat something, Vere.'

'How many oranges?'

'Just the one.'

'I think I could eat another.'

'Finish this one first.'

But Vere is sick before he finishes.

'No more oranges for you, my lad,' comments the nurse. A day or two later she leaves. Vere immediately shows a slight improvement. One evening his father comes into his room and says he is going away.

'When, Dad?'

'Tomorrow.'

'Tomorrow! Where?'

'Abroad, America.'

'For a long time?'

'Yes, quite a time. When I get back you'll be as fit as a fiddle.'

The idea of this departure, although he has scarcely seen his father since his illness began, horrifies Vere. He wants nothing to change: he cannot bear that it should. He feels that an opportunity which he has privately treasured but never properly attempted to realise is slipping through his fingers: he feels because of his weakness that he can no longer observe the niceties which in the past have smothered his relations with his father: unprepared as he is, he still feels forced to take his chance.

'Dad,' he says, 'do you remember when you shot the pigeon?'

'What made you think of that?'

'I think of it often.'

'Do you?'

'Yes. Do you remember when we walked home, Dad?'

'Why?'

'It was dark, wasn't it? I loved that evening.'

The tears come into his eyes. He cannot master them any more: he seems to be made of tears. Sentimental and unsatisfying, they spoil his good intentions.

'Take us shooting when you come home, Dad.'

'Yes, Vere, yes, I will.'

'I wish you weren't going.'

'So do I.'

'You couldn't shoot the pigeon, could you, Dad – to begin with?'

'No,' his father smiles.

'But then you did, I knew you would. And we walked home together . . .' He is ruining everything with his senseless repetition. 'Leo and I ate the pigeon.' The tears run down his cheeks. He loved that pigeon – why did he eat it? How sad, how sad! 'Oh, Dad, I wish you weren't going away . . .' Although untrue, the expression of this wish again makes the tears start. Everything is too difficult; he is too tired. However hard he may grip his father's thumb with his moist hand he still cannot touch him. And he cannot explain. It is easier to dwell on the mere fact of his father's departure and to let the misunderstood tears flow. 'I wish you weren't going, Dad . . .'

'It won't be for long, monkey. We'll have a celebration when I get back. And you're better anyway. Don't cry – come on, old boy, come on now.'

A big silk handkerchief is produced which smells of tobacco. Vere wipes his eyes, sees his father's concerned face, tries to apologise for the tears he feels he has inflicted upon him, cries again. At length he controls himself.

'I'll send you some post-cards.'

'Thank you, Dad.'

'Mummy's going to get the vet in if you're not well soon.'

'Is she, Dad?'

'Well . . . Goodbye, monkey.'

'Have a nice time, Dad.'

Lips a little pursed and head bent forward his father leaves the room. Vere lies drained and exhausted after he has gone, studying the firelight on the smooth ceiling.

Healing dreamless sleep claims him that night and the following nights. He wakes calmly from his slumbers, soon grows drowsy again, slips into cool sleep, once more wakes. His illness is over. It is as if the tears he shed with his bewildered father contained all the poison and pain in his system. He begins to anticipate his meals, to demand amusement. He leaves his bed for the first time, protesting, and gloomily sits beside it for an hour. The next day he sits gloomily for two hours, but when he climbs back into bed is hot and restless. The third day he eats his tea in the nursery and has to be persuaded to return to his bedroom. He is wheeled out-of-doors in the old wickerwork bath-chair. He plans complex routes and time-tables which he follows closely, shouting directions to Flora while he grips the long steering-arm and consults his father's stop-watch. He lives from hour to hour, from day to day, happy with the happiness that is in the song of the cold robin, wistful, fleeting, borne hither and thither on the blustery wind, rising, falling, heard and unheard.

He is to go to the seaside with Nanny. On the morning of the day before he is due to leave he receives a letter from Leo. 'I am glad you are better,' his brother writes. 'We will share a room when you come to school next autumn. It will be great fun . . .'

After breakfast on the same day Karen tells him privately that Flora is going to be married. Although he can foresee no way in which this will affect him, for some reason Vere neither questions Karen on the subject nor mentions it to Flora.

That afternoon, for the last time, Flora wheels him out in the bath-chair. Halfway down the front-drive they come across old Harris the gardener, sitting on the handle of his wheelbarrow in the lee of the garden wall. Vere steers the bath-chair alongside and greets him, then, noticing a short black pipe held in his knobbly hand, happens to ask after Mr Bruise who possesses a corn-cob pipe that is nine years old.

'Mr Bruise?' Harris lifts his worn tweed hat and drops it back on his head. 'He's bad, they tell me, Master Vere. Nice afternoon, isn't it?'

'What do you mean he's bad, Mr Harris?'

'Ill, I mean, after his operation.'

Vere looks at Flora. 'Has Mr Bruise been ill? I didn't know.'

'Yes, sweetheart. Come along.'

'It's all right, Flora, I've allowed us lots of time. When did he have his operation?' Vere asks idly.

'That was just after Christmas. He was poorly a good bit.'

'Is he better now?'

'They say he's bad, I've not been up there.'

Vere glances at the stop-watch in his lap. Now they are behind their schedule.

'Is he able to eat?' Flora is asking.

'He's this here pipe in his throat. Poor old man, he won't last winter. He can't take no nourishment.'

'What sort of pipe?' Vere inquires curiously, imagining for a moment that the words must refer in some way to Mr Bruise's corn-cob.

But Flora interrupts. 'Give him my kind regards, Mr Harris, if you see him. Good afternoon. Which way, Vere?'

'Down the drive, turn left,' he answers. After they have creaked along for a bit he asks, 'What does it mean, Flora?'

'Nothing, sweetheart. How are we getting on?'

'We're late.' He raises his voice: 'But you must tell me, Flora. I understood.'

'Mr Bruise went into hospital, sweetheart, and they found out there was something wrong with his throat, that's all.'

'And they put a pipe in it – in his throat?' He emphasises the words strongly.

'Yes.'

'Why?'

'Well, so he could swallow.'

The wheelchair bumps and trundles over the ruts. In an angry tone Vere continues. 'Do they feed him through this pipe?'

'Yes, but don't ask me any more about it.'

'Where is the pipe?' he returns in his angry tone.

'I've told you, Vere.'

'But how do they feed him? And what with?'

'Now, Vere.'

'Tell me, Flora.' She does not answer. 'Flora!' His heart thumps. 'I can find out easily, don't worry.' Flora says nothing.

They turn left at the bottom of the dipping drive, left again up the back-drive.

Flora says, 'I don't know more than I've told you, Vere.'

'Is Mr Bruise going to die?' Vere asks sadly.

'He's very ill, that's all we know, sweetheart.'

By the greenhouses they again meet Harris. He lifts his crumpled hat a second time and exposes a bald white head. Vere calls to Flora to stop.

'Mr Harris,' he says. 'If you see Mr Bruise . . .' He shudders and looks away. 'Will you tell him I've been ill?'

'Yes, Master Vere. He likes news of the family, always did.'

'Mr Harris, can he smoke?'

'I don't expect he can.'

'I wonder what's happened to his corn-cob.'

'He'll be missing that.'

'Goodbye, Mr Harris. I'm going away tomorrow.'

'You get well then, Master Vere. Goodbye.'

Flora pushes the bath-chair along the cinder-path and asks which way to go.

'Just home, Flora,' he replies.

Vere does not think again of Mr Bruise, of school or Flora's marriage. A merciful gauze descends and surrounds him, softening the hard edges of unpleasant facts, blunting their sharp implications. He leaves for his holiday without noticing Flora's strained looks when she bids him goodbye and the unwonted warmth of her final hug.

Nanny and Vere spend ten days by the seaside. Gradually

the colour floods back into the boy's cheeks. He eats enormously and after the first two days refuses to be wheeled in the battered bath-chair. Morning and afternoon he goes for lengthening walks along the front with Nanny. He breathes the keen salty air, watches the rough green sea, wishes he lived by the seaside. In the evenings, in their bedroom which smells of sand and rubber shoes, Nanny and he sit by the fire over a jig-saw puzzle or a game of Old Maid. The days pass in a happy blur: they are unpacking, they are packing: Albert arrives to fetch them home.

During the drive, at first regretful, then excited, Nanny says, 'Vere, I want to warn you that Flora's leaving us.'

'For her holiday?' he asks.

'No. She's to be married.'

'Oh yes.' He nods. Then he says incredulously, 'She's not going away?'

'I'm afraid she is.'

'When?'

'She'll be leaving tomorrow. She's being married the day after and she'll spend the night at Long Cretton.'

'I see,' he says.

Later he says, 'I never thought she'd have to go away.'

'She's going to live at Long Cretton. You'll be able to visit her quite often.'

'Does she want to leave us?' he inquires.

'Well, she wants to get married.'

'What's her husband's name?'

'Rodney Marston.'

'I see,' he says again.

At home everybody is delighted with the changes in Vere's appearance. He is full of his holiday, spends the remainder of the day describing it, and only remembers Flora's impending departure after he has gone to bed. The next morning, before leaving for school, Mary and Karen come to say goodbye to Flora who is wearing a new dress. When they have left Nanny takes Faith into the night-nursery.

'Sweetheart,' Flora says as Vere makes for the door into the passage, 'I think I'd better be saying goodbye.'

Vere, who has assumed that Flora would be staying until lunchtime anyway, stops and asks in a shocked voice, 'Now?'

'I've lots of things to do in Cretton,' Flora explains.

'Oh, all right,' he says grudgingly, then, gaining time in which to steel himself for this vaguely threatening scene, he inquires, 'Flora, whereabouts in Cretton are you going to live?'

'We've a bungalow. It's just off the High Street. Will you come and see us, Vere?'

'Yes, I will.'

Flora's dress is dark blue with a white collar and white cuffs. Her face is white too, he notices. And her eyes are huge, pale, abstracted but searching.

'What's your house called?' he asks quickly.

'Well,' she smiles, 'it's a funny name. Little Lodge.'

'Little Lodge. Yes,' he smiles in reply, thinking, What is the matter with Flora? She is making everything so strange and difficult – she is even speaking strangely. He wishes she would say goodbye. He feels that the veil which has protected him since he learnt of Mr Bruise's illness is in danger of being parted, being rent. And he clings to his veil. Afraid of emotions which have betrayed and pained him in the recent past, he does not want to feel strongly – he does not want to feel more than wistful and melancholy. Goodbye, Flora, he says to himself: I love you, Flora: later, later I will feel sad: but now, goodbye.

Aloud he says, 'I'll come often and see you, Flora, it's not really like saying goodbye,' hoping thus to belittle their parting, to make of it a light and trifling affair.

'No, it's not like saying goodbye,' Flora repeats after him, and there is a pause.

He stands by the combined cupboard and chest of drawers, Flora by the dresser in between the windows. The budgerigars scratch on the sanded floor of their house-like cage at the end of the low room. It is a grey day. He steals a glance at Flora, but hastily looks away. Surely her eyes were shining unnaturally? Although uncertain he dare not look again. She cannot – must not cry. He starts to panic. He does not know what to say, he cannot abide this heavy silence. The door of the scrubbed-oak cupboard suddenly swings open. He laughs.

'Look,' he says with relief, banging the door. But again it swings open.

'Where's the piece of paper that wedges it?'

'I don't know.'

Flora crosses the room. He wishes he could see that piece of paper, find and replace it. Flora's nearness adds to his panic. If only she were still by the dresser, still at a distance! He kneels, making as much as he can of the movement, and lowers his head until his eye is level with the floor.

'I've got it,' Flora says above him, 'it was in the cupboard,' and she wedges the door.

Vere straightens up. But his exertions have released some essential spring of his control. His legs shake, he feels brittle, as if at the least jar he will break, and also exposed, undefended. And the tension steadily mounts. He holds his breath. All depends on Flora, he is at her mercy. Not that same sadness, not that pain – not again, Flora, he prays.

'Sweetheart,' she speaks in an ordinary voice and pauses. Her back is turned to him – neat dark head, white collar – and her hand rests on a ledge of the cupboard door – supporting her, it seems, holding her up. 'What am I going to do without you, Vere?'

She turns. Her blue eyes swim with tears and her lower lip trembles.

'How will I get on, Vere? I don't know. I don't know how I'll manage at all.'

He seizes her hands, her firm arms, her neck above the white collar. She bends down and embraces him.

'I've made you cry. And I didn't mean to. There, sweetheart, don't, don't.' But she is crying so much that she speaks indistinctly. 'I'm going.'

'No, Flora.'

'I must.'

'Nanny and Faith . . .'

'Not now.'

'Please, Flora . . .'

'Goodbye, sweetheart, goodbye, Vere.' She opens the

passage door. 'Come and see me soon,' she says, stumbles down the two steps and passes out of sight.

Vere remains by the scrubbed-oak cupboard for some time, then goes and sits on the window-seat. He wipes his eyes with a handkerchief that still smells of the seaside, and remembers his father's handkerchief that smelt of tobacco when last he wiped his eyes. Recalling those paltry tears he smiles: never before has he felt so sad. And thinking of Flora he continues to cry and to stare through the window.

But now it is an entirely new sadness, not peculiar or clinging, neither senseless nor exhausting, that causes Vere's heart to ache. Although he feels sad all over, even in his feet and the tips of his fingers, he is free, and his spirit is clear as it has not been for many months. His fears scatter. He opens his heart to life, and his true sadness, faithful, looking forward, liberating, swells within him.

He is well.

SIX

SPRING AND SUMMER

Winter passes and spring comes. Under the influence of the spring sun and air Vere's health improves; and like the light which changes perceptibly, becoming ever finer in quality, more colourful and of a softer, sweeter texture, he too feels himself changing. Once more his mood matches the mood of the season. The snowdrops in the drive, the daffodils, the first green of the trees, the clear evenings which lengthen: these transformations of atmosphere and landscape reflect the processes taking place inside himself. The spring is his own: he unfolds with it: yet as the spring anticipates the summer, so he, with hope and fear, anticipates time that is still to come.

For now Vere's life is overshadowed by the endless and insuperable cliff of school. All his fancies are limited by that dread finality, all his activities curtailed by it. He is conscious of the months that remain to him: he is no longer carefree: the simple present does not satisfy: the future is not forever. Filled with longings, sweet and languorous, for some mysterious happening – some vague but beautiful happening – which will disperse this black shadow, which like sunlight will dazzle and blind, he waits, he hopes, and his expectant hours become days, his days weeks, his weeks fortnights and precious months.

In search of his beautiful happening he recalls the old days. But Flora is gone – and Edith the housemaid who does her work cannot replace her – his father is abroad: nothing can ever be the same. Yet what times they had, how happy they were! He thinks of Leo's birthday, of the moment under the nut-hedge. The holidays are approaching and he thinks of Leo often. He is convinced that his brother will be struck by his many new qualities – his increased understanding and affection, for instance: and he feels that if only he can confide in Leo as he never has before – really reveal and explain himself – their friendship is bound to become tender and true. And since he reaches out towards truth, towards tenderness, towards love and trust, and the absorbing joy that they will bring, he awaits his brother's return with impatience and devouring hope.

Leo arrives. Vere moves his mattress into his brother's bedroom and sleeps on the floor for five nights. There are jokes and happy laughter, enjoyable tussles and fights, even the occasional conversation, but he does not confide in Leo. Something always seems to prevent him from doing so, some joke or inattention on his brother's part. In the end their constant laughter, unravelling and then disintegrating, makes Vere feel weak when he remembers the onus of his intricate explanation. Overcome by a sense of futility and failure, of disappointment and dissatisfaction, he is not sorry to return to his comfortable bed.

The brothers have decided to build a house. Vere believes that the work will unite them, that as they near the supreme moment of completion the confidential climate must improve, and that once he has spoken frankly to Leo their relationship will enter into its desired phase. With liberal use of the word Jackson the house is planned. Leo's conception of it is grand, radical: Vere's, by comparison, modest and rather dull. Vere quotes from his experience, but Leo sweeps aside difficulties as if they did not exist. He insists on some means of heating their house. Vere says he has considered this before but found it impracticable – 'What sort of a fire, Leo, and where do you think you 're going to get it?' he asks. By way of answer Leo requisitions the stove in the old potting-shed, blithely informing his mother of the fact some days afterwards. To start with Vere is delighted by Leo's ruthless methods, his knack of obtaining what he wants almost before he has decided if he wants it. But when he orders planks from the local timber-merchant, Vere, discovering that he is expected to pay half their cost, cannot help feeling that the whole principle of building houses is being betrayed. There is nothing secret about Leo's house, nothing personal or magic – it is a house: he makes no attempt to adapt materials to his uses, does not employ ingenuity, does not contrive – he buys or borrows what he needs, requests aid and suggestions from everybody, is always ready to discuss the project. And this approach of Leo's palls on Vere. He ceases to contribute his usually despised ideas and waits for the actual physical labour which he finds so pleasant to begin.

But here again there is trouble. Leo starts with a flourish, working throughout the day, and only Vere's pride prevents him from begging for a respite. The next day Leo works intermittently, pausing often to admire Vere's concentration and craftsmanship. The third day he wants to bicycle into Long Cretton. Vere dissuades him and they return to the house, but Leo picks holes in everything they have so far achieved and expresses doubts as to whether they should in any case continue. Vere is shocked, the brothers quarrel, and for some days Vere works alone: then Leo apologises and proceeds to take an enormous amount of trouble over the positioning and lighting of the rusty stove. Eventually the house is finished. But although it is more solid than any of Vere's other houses, although it has a bright crackling fire, and is watertight and windtight, and a real object of admiration, it affords him scant pleasure. Leo's attitude – his lack of interest, unequal bouts of labour, inconsistency and public ways – seems to have rendered the whole undertaking hollow and meaningless.

The brothers are sitting in the house one morning when Leo says, 'Pretty good bit of work we've done here, Jackson.'

'Yes,' Vere replies, picking a dry twig from the heap beside the stove and cracking it in his fingers.

'Lovely and warm and snug, isn't it?'

'Yes,' Vere agrees, poking the twig into the red roaring fire.

'What can we do now?'

Leo is always wondering what he can do.

'Well, we can sit and talk. And we might build a sort of outhouse.'

'Oh don't let's build any more.'

'Well, we could . . .' But Vere suddenly feels tired of devising amusements for Leo. He recalls his dream of friendship with his brother. Because he has strayed so far from it – down the old hopeless path, he realises: permitting Leo to dictate, resenting his dictation – he answers angrily, 'I don't know what we can do.'

Leo appears not to notice. He clicks his tongue and says, 'There's never anything to do here. Let's ring up Tim.' Tim is his school friend.

'Go ahead,' says Vere.

'Well, what are we going to do?'

Vere gazes at the rough stakes in the wall of the house, and craning his neck unnaturally, at the dark planks of the roof. 'You don't want to stay here, Leo, do you?' he says bitterly. 'Just stay here, I mean, quietly, and do things here?' He glances at his brother, whose blue-green eyes are cool and critical.

'What are you talking about?'

'Nothing, Leo.'

'We built the house together, didn't we?'

'A fat lot of building you did.' He thrusts his finger into a knot-hole in one of the planks. He is not sure if he is confiding in Leo or denouncing him. He is only sure that he is making a fool of himself.

'Go away, baby,' says Leo.

'All right, I will.' Vere rises to his feet.

'Sit down and stop being so silly.'

But Vere walks out of the house.

Leo announces at luncheon that Tim is coming to tea. Turning to Vere he says, 'Is my baby brother feeling better?' Vere does not answer. He scarcely speaks for two days. He cannot surmount his sense of grievance. Tim comes to tea with Leo, Leo goes to tea with Tim. The brothers' house is dismantled by the gardeners.

For some time after this episode Vere is very cautious and reserved in his dealings with Leo. But towards the end of the holidays, securely armoured as he feels himself to be, he relaxes his tight defences. One morning – always a tricky period where Leo is concerned – he is reading an interesting book in the nursery when his brother again asks what they can do.

Vere ignores the question. Leo repeats it. Vere replies that he is reading. Leo proposes they should take a walk. Vere remains silent. Leo begins to taunt him. Vere pretends not to hear.

'Afraid to get your feet wet? Frightened of the fresh air? It'll make you look a bit more healthy. You don't understand that book so I don't know why you're reading. Jump into the pram and I'll wheel you into the garden.'

'Leo,' Vere says reasonably, 'why don't you go out alone?'

'Oh, I wouldn't dare without you to protect me. Come on, baby.'

'Don't call me baby, Leo, and please leave me alone.'

Leo crawls across the floor and starts to tickle Vere's legs. Vere changes his position: Leo follows him: he goes into the night-nursery, his finger marking the place in his book.

Leo inquires, 'Ready for bed? I'll fetch your pyjamas.' Vere proceeds into the next room, bangs the door and leans against it. Leo pushes. Vere jumps away and his brother falls forward: he laughs and sits down on a chair.

'Trying to be funny, are you?' says Leo, 'I'll tell you a good joke,' and he snatches away the book.

Roused at last Vere demands its immediate return. Leo laughs successfully and runs away. Vere chases him all over the house, catches him, hits him twice on the shoulder as hard as he can, then picks up the book which has been thrown aside, dodges into his mother's bathroom and locks the door. Leo, pained by the blows, loses his temper. He hammers on the door, looks through the keyhole, shouts insults through it, swears that he will not budge until Vere comes out. But his temper never lasts and soon he is laughing and enjoying himself.

Too angry to wait for Leo to tire of this sport Vere silently raises the bottom sash of the bathroom window and looks out. There is a drop of twenty feet onto the paving-stones of the backyard, but a few feet to the right of the window-sill is the sloping slated roof of the nursery-passage. If he were able to reach that roof he could climb along it and get into the house by one of the passage windows. And whilst Leo continued to thump on the door of the empty bathroom, he would be free to read undisturbed in the nursery. In spite of his rage he is sourly amused by his crafty and audacious plan. He stuffs the book into his pocket and swings himself out of the window.

He is less amused when he tries to straighten his knees: less still when he realises he cannot reach the roof with his outstretched leg. He will have to jump. But now the paving-stones look grim: and he notices that some of the slates on the roof are perilously loose. 'Having a bath, baby?' he hears Leo call. 'Come out and I'll give you a present – something you'll remember. Come out, little man. Come out, you sulky boy.' He shifts his balance to the outstretched leg and shoves himself sideways and backwards with the aid of a drainpipe. He seems to waver in mid-air for a second – his heart shrinks to the size of a pea and his scalp pricks – then his foot touches the roof. On all fours he slithers over the slates as quick as he can, squeezes through a window, tiptoes into the nursery, resumes his initial seat, produces his book and once more finds his place.

He is much too angry to read. The book shakes in his hands and the words swim. Now his heart is swollen – distended with anger. He has been stripped of his armour, goaded into this destroying frenzy, into risking danger, into suffering fear – at Leo's will, for Leo's pleasure. He smarts from ancient hurts, revives injustices. With shame he recalls his mistaken hopes of friendship with his brother. Schemes of revenge swarm in his throbbing head. He forgets that he has won the day – but it is not today for which he wishes to revenge himself – rises to his feet and stalks stiffly down the nursery passage, intent on dealing Leo a final, absolute and crushing defeat.

Leo is still shouting and banging on the bathroom door. Vere watches him for a moment, then says, 'Do you want anyone, Leo?' But he is so terribly angry that he sounds as if he is sobbing.

Leo turns. Instead of the unguarded surprise Vere hoped to see in his flushed face there is only cold hostility. 'Hullo, baby,' he says. Suddenly he laughs. 'I knew you'd get out, baby.'

Vere answers cuttingly, 'It's not hard to get away from you.' But again the sentence sounds like a sob.

'Anyone can get through that window.'

'It made you look a pretty good fool.'

'Why are you crying?'

'I'm not.'

'You'll have to go back and unlock the door.'

'I won't.'

'I don't mind. Anyway, it's lunchtime.' Leo laughs again, unexpectedly ruffles Vere's hair as he passes him, and runs along to the nursery.

Vere remains where he is – his hair disordered, tears of powerless anger in his eyes – outside the bathroom door. He longs to follow Leo, to catch, to beat, to pummel him. He is prevented by his anger, which calls for deeper satisfaction. Yet in no serious way – only by force – can he touch, let alone crush, his laughing brother. Bitterly he accuses Leo of his many crimes; but more bitterly he reproaches himself for his inability to convict or to punish him.

None of the wrathful arrows Vere continues to aim at Leo finds its mark: in fact they rebound off Leo's tough hide and wound Vere. He retires into miserable silence. Albert has to fetch a ladder in order to open the bathroom door. Since Vere refuses to explain what has happened he is blamed for causing Albert trouble. For several days he does not speak to Leo. He is repeatedly told to forgive and forget, but he cannot, and is blamed for this also. He relents only on the morning that Leo goes to school. It is the last time he will say goodbye to his brother: at the end of the next holidays he will accompany him. Alone once more, he is nervous and depressed, his numbered days overshadowed, his hopes proscribed. But the lovely weather soothes and consoles him, and gradually he begins to sort out, to piece together and to weigh, the hurried experience of the past four weeks.

And he cannot understand anything. He cannot understand

why Leo is not the friend he desires; why his ready love for Leo was refused; why he hates Leo. He cannot remember how he came to entertain such thoughts about his brother. He cannot understand Leo's wounding strength, his own apparent weakness. He cannot understand his error. He dreamed of magic happenings, of joy, of friendship – then of Leo. He dreamed of Leo: that was his mistake. For Leo is as he has always been: he does not change. It was the change in Vere – his vain and vulnerable dream – which brought about his present injuries. But this he does not understand.

And because he does not understand he goes on dreaming. He is not sad. He spends much of his time with Nanny. Since Flora's departure she has become the pivot of his life. With her he can be true to himself as she is true. His confidence is always respected. But he does not try to speak to her of what concerns him most closely: he could not speak of it: and his silence, his recognition of the fact that explanation is unnecessary between them, is a measure of his love and trust, for with other people he often feels a pressing and fatal need to explain himself. Nanny is his friend in the same way that his right hand is his friend. Mal is his friend and Flora at Long Cretton is his dear friend. And after all he is happy with his friends. He is happy that he can run in the sunlit garden, can sit by Nanny's wicker-work chair under the apple trees, can play with Faith, can shout and laugh and look for birds'-nests in the thick hedges. But where none-the-less he wonders, where, where – is that peculiar friend his heart craves? Where is that happiness he can hold shining, like a nugget of gold, between his hands? Why, in spite of his friends, does he feel solitary? And in spite of his happiness sad? Ah, one day, one day . . . He will come on this extraordinary happiness of which he dreams. He will dig it up like buried treasure. He will shower it richly on his perfect friend, on all his friends, on all the people he has ever met, on all the people in all the world. Everyone will be happy and he will be happiest of all. The days will be composed of moments like the one under the nut-hedge on Leo's last birthday – a series of similar moments, strung everlastingly together: the nights will be starry and blue. And soon he will find this happiness, soon he will find his friend.

Vere dreams and the days pass. His few months of future are being whittled away. In order not to look forward to what is terrible, he hopes for his mysterious happening – how he hopes! – through May, through June. He does not know the form that it will take, he does not know from what quarter to expect it – there is still no sign: he believes in it more firmly. He cannot bear to do otherwise. But time is always passing. He grows impatient, fretful. Summer comes. His mother leaves for America. One day Vere receives a letter from his father.

'Dear old boy,' his father writes. 'Mummy has arrived safely with all the news from home and has made me feel very homesick. It must be glorious now, isn't it? Warm sunny days, I expect, so different from here. I wish I was with you. Do you remember when we shot the pigeon? It was fun, wasn't it? We'll go shooting again when I get back. It looks as if I may have to leave earlier than planned. So looking forward to seeing you, dear old man – Daddy.'

Vere reads and rereads this letter, keeps it in his breast pocket, sleeps with it under his pillow.

His father will be the friend for whom he has waited.

SEVEN

A HUNT AND KILL

Vere is in his father's bedroom – out-of-bounds to the children – when his parents arrive home.

It is an evening in late August. More than half the holidays have gone. The cliff of school menaces now, and Vere's dreams have become confused. Sometimes it seems as if he is climbing up a steep path known only to himself – climbing and climbing up this secret path, by means of which he is avoiding all the fears and frightful dangers of the cliff, and that soon he will emerge into brightest sunlight. But he cannot climb any higher without help from his father, without love and kind understanding. And now he is about to receive this help. He still does not know the exact form that it will take. He believes simply that it will be different from anything he has ever known; that his father will be different; that his mother, everyone will be different; that his life will change; that dread will be quite removed; that certain joy will replace it. Sometimes it seems as if only a few yards of dark path separate him from this sunny upland: more often though his dreams are clouded by anxiety.

He sits in the single chair in his father's bedroom and strains his ears. He is sure he will hear the car. A myriad indefinable outdoor noises float through the open windows. Pleasant thrills begin to run up his spine. His father will soon be home. He leans back in the chair and opens the cupboard door. The owner of so many clothes, hanging suits and pairs of tilted shoes, must needs be a different and extraordinary person.

Rising to his feet he goes over to the mirror and tries to smile gently, crinkling his eyes. It occurs to him that his imagination never carries him beyond his father's gentle smile. He makes a face like a monkey, then like a Chinaman. He starts to laugh silently, in a loose excited way, when suddenly, to his astonishment, he hears voices in the hall and steps on the front stairs.

He stops laughing and his heart beats very fast. All his serious hopes soar to a climax. Without thinking he runs out of the bedroom.

'Darling!' his mother says, reaching the landing and giving him a kiss.

His father, who also gives him a kiss, says with a frown, 'What were you doing in my room, you little rat?'

For a moment Vere is unable to speak. Nothing – nothing has changed. His parents look the same, wear the same clothes, say the same things in the same voices, kiss as they have always kissed. They might never have been away. Rather than being as he imagined and hoped, everything is as he has tried not to remember it. And his father's smile, of which he has thought so often, is like a barrier between them – just as it used to be: as it has always been, he now remembers. He manages to say, 'I didn't know you were here.'

'We've been in the garden with the others. You have grown, darling! Are you well?'

'Yes, Mummy, thank you.'

'But why were you in my room?' His father smiles but is obviously not pleased. 'You mustn't go in there.'

Vere smiles too, but cannot meet his father's eye.

'Were you in Daddy's room?' his mother asks, puffing at a cigarette. 'Well, shall we go along and see Faith?'

'All right, Mummy. She was waiting for you.'

'Oh, there's the new carpet,' says his father, pointing along the passage.

Vere follows his parents to the nursery. He blames the bedroom for everything. No more is said about it. He draws his mother's attention to this, his father's to that, hoping to make them forget the incident, but as a result he feels deceitful, and suffers from his old painful sense of nothing being either complete or clear.

He is relieved when they go downstairs. In the smoking-room his parents open their letters, tearing the envelopes and throwing them onto the floor, while the children loll on the sofa, talking in whispers. From time to time a remark is addressed to them – 'What are you up to?' 'We won't be long, darlings' – then more envelopes are torn and tossed aside. But the charming room with its shelves of unread books, beautifully bound, its shiny cushions, tall lamps and dulled discreet looking-glass – this harmonious room has never seemed to Vere more enclosed, and he believes that if he could only get out of it, passing through the wide french windows into the airy garden, he would feel a hundred times better and all things would again become possible.

In a way he is right. At length the family moves through the windows. The children chatter and hang on the arms of their parents, who listen abstractedly, smoking and smiling. Vere feels suddenly full of energy – like a piece of twisted elastic – and runs and leaps to everyone's amusement. But he is still dissatisfied. Whenever he pauses he looks questioningly at his father, and the winks and quacking noises he receives in answer are like added twists to the elastic inside him, which only a fresh series of wild leaps, hops and bursts of laughter on the part of the beholders, can unwind. Now he blames the clothes his father is wearing for his dissatisfaction – that diamond pin in his black tie, those pointed black shoes, the stiff collar and the blue suit. Now he blames the desired stroll through the garden, now the fact that he is not alone with his father. All the same he begins to feel better. And later in the evening, when he goes to bed, it seems to him that he is nearing the summit of his hard path.

Several days pass. One afternoon Vere comes across his father in the garden. He looks up from the seat on which he is sitting and says lazily, 'Well, monkey – what are you so busy about? Come and sit down.'

Vere starts to excuse himself. 'I was just going to the potting-shed,' he says, gesturing as if to emphasise the importance of his mission. But then, recollecting his dreams, he changes his mind. 'Oh – perhaps I will sit down,' he says, feeling clumsy and self-conscious.

'Isn't it lovely?' says his father.

'Yes,' Vere replies, and there is a long pause. He keeps on thinking of things to say, but none of them seems suitable and he remains silent. He knows that this is his opportunity, yet all he can do is stretch his toes with embarrassment and wait. The hot sunlight stupefies him. He gazes at a baked flowerbed and grows unreasonably angry.

'Why were you going to the potting-shed?' his father asks at length, lowering his head and leaning forward with his elbows on his knees.

'To get a saw,' Vere answers briefly, feeling that his father is not interested, that the question is beside the point.

'What do you want with a saw?'

'We're building a sort of cart, Leo and me.'

There is another pause. Covertly Vere regards the back of his father's head, the smooth hair curling crisply at the ends and the red neck with its pale furrows. Now that he cannot see his father's face he is free to imagine its expression: a kind expression, he is sure, and gentle, frank – the sort of expression he has often imagined in the past. His anger leaves him and he waits patiently, his mind revolving round his hopes and fancies, while the sunlight eases his constraint. All will be well: he cannot worry: he wishes his hair curled like his father's: he wishes he was like his father – had the same strong neck and big hands: he loves his father, they will be friends: it is too hot to worry anyway.

Without looking up his father says, 'What about school, old boy?'

The question seems to match Vere's mood so closely, seems to him so wonderfully intimate, that his heart, instead of sinking as it usually does at the mention of the word 'school', bounds upward. He replies 'I know,' but the two senseless words express for the first time a little of all he is feeling and longs to convey.

'When is it, the sixteenth of September?'

'Yes.'

'I'll have to come and see you.'

'Will you really?'

'We'll go out fishing in the sea, would you like that?'

'Yes, Dad, I would.'

'I took Leo last year.'

'Did you?'

Vere digests the information about Leo, determined not to let it mar his tentative happiness, then says, 'How old were you when you went to school, Dad?'

His father turns his head and glances out of the corner of his eye. 'About the same age as you. Why?'

'Well . . .' Vere pauses. The expression on his father's face is not at all as he imagined it. He studies the flowerbed, trying to forget that cold suspicious glance. Then he dismisses his fears. He tells himself that he is nearing the summit of his path, that his exertions are about to be rewarded; and so he ignores the warning signs, braces himself as if for a last effort, and speaks out.

'Dad, did you mind going to school?' he inquires.

'What?' His father sounds surprised. He stirs restlessly and continues with a half-laugh. 'Yes, I suppose I did a bit.' He lifts his head and leans against the back of the creaking lichened seat. 'But you don't mind, do you?' he asks.

Vere looks at his father, says 'No,' and rises quickly to his feet.

'Where are you off to?'

'I'd better get the saw.'

'Be careful with it, won't you?'

'Yes.'

As Vere walks away he hears the click of his father's cigarette-case and the rasp of a match, and he thinks, angrily, again, How can he smoke? That his father should calmly smoke after what has happened seems dreadful to him. He feels suddenly hopeless and unhappy.

More even than Vere suspected hung on his question about school. He does not understand why he answered his father in the negative, but he knows he could not have answered otherwise. If only his father had said, 'Yes, I minded. Do you mind?' – if only he had said that, Vere could have spoken of what acutely concerns him and everything would have been transformed. Truth would have removed fear, love fulfilled hollow dreams. But his father did not ask or want to know whether Vere minded: he merely wanted Vere to say that he did not mind. His words, the tone of his voice, his expression, the movement of his hands – all made it plain that he required a certain unencumbering reply.

'You don't mind, do you?'

'No.'

To Vere, perched on his craggy and perilous path, that enforced concealment of the truth is like a blow on the head. He cried out to his father, released his precarious hold, reached upwards – he was so near the summit, so very close. He received no help. Therefore he falls, falls and is bruised, and an avalanche of hopes, of dreams, tumbles down on top of him.

His grand feelings for his father begin to resemble his old feelings for Leo. The cherished thoughts of many weeks cannot be wiped away at will. Although they shame him, an affectionate smile from his father or a kind word – the least demonstration is enough to prove, by the involuntary surge of longing and joy it produces, that he is not free of them. He pretends that he does not care; avoids his father; is cautious and reserved; forgets his fantasy about the path. But his hopeless and unhappy feeling steadily increases.

And the days flit by. Happening to pass the stable archway one afternoon Vere notices a commotion in the cobbled yard and goes to investigate. A little mare called Contact has arrived on trial for his father. She is a nervous animal, black, with a muscular neck and small head, and delicate tapering legs. After she has been stabled and the grooms have dispersed, Vere, possessed by one of those whims to which he is liable nowadays, begs a couple of apples from the head-groom and approaches the door of the loose-box. The mare swings round when he calls, and with nodding head moves towards him. He balances one of the apples in the palm of his hand and holds it out.

'Here, Contact, come on, Contact. Now don't bite me,' he murmurs.

The mare extends her head, eyes slanting curiously, breathes warm air onto Vere's hand through dilating nostrils, then nibbles the apple into her mouth with her soft mobile lips. Her yellow teeth show for an instant; she munches once, tosses her head, and stares at something on the other side of the yard. Delighted by her gentle ways and knowing expression, Vere offers Contact the second apple.

This is the start of a strange friendship which develops during the next few days between the boy and the little mare. Had he stopped to think Vere would have been surprised by his constant visits to the stables, of which he usually steers clear, and his complete absence of fear in all his dealings with Contact, when he has never before been anything but frightened of horses. But he does not stop to think, and his undemanding tenderness affords him relief from the intricate consideration of his feelings for his father. Perhaps the very oddness of the object on which he chooses to lavish his love and countless attentions stimulates him; perhaps he feels that the mare's unsettled future and his own are intertwined; perhaps he senses some sad dumb fellowship between them. Whatever the reason may be, the moments he spends clinging to the top of the loose-box door, talking to Contact, stroking and feeding her, become for him the most real and precious moments of this period.

On two occasions his father gallops the mare in the field by the back-drive. Sitting on the stone stile in the wall Vere watches proudly as she trots over the close grass, canters with a free but restrained grace, and finally gallops, hinting at her speed and well-knit strength.

On the way back to the stables after the second gallop Vere asks his father, whom he seems able to meet on this neutral ground, if he is going to keep the mare.

'I want to try her out with hounds first,' his father answers. 'I thought I might take her cubbing tomorrow.'

'Can I come, Dad?'

'Well, the meet's pretty early.'

'I don't mind.'

'Do you want to come, you monkey?'

'Yes, very much.'

'Well, we'll see.'

'And then you'll buy her, won't you, Dad?'

'I may. Do you like her?'

'Yes.'

Later in the day the subject of the cub-hunting is again broached by Vere. The other children join him in begging to be allowed to go. Permission is granted and Mal agrees to accompany them.

That evening Vere takes somc lumps of sugar out to Contact. He steals across the deserted yard, peeps over the high door of the loose-box and whispers her name. The mare pricks her ears, turns, rustling the thick straw that covers her hooves, and comes towards him.

'What do you want?' he teases her, stepping back and showing his empty hands. 'I haven't anything for you. What is it then?'

The mare presses her nose against his chest, breathing gently. 'No, I haven't anything. Honestly I haven't,' he says, putting his hands in his pockets.

Contact raises her head and appears to lose interest.

'Contact!' he commands. She pays no attention. 'Why Contact,' he says in a sly voice, 'guess what I've found. Look at that, well I never.'

She dips her head and nuzzles his closed fist. He opens it gradually, and as she takes the sugar slips into his favourite position, his back against the door of the loose-box, the mare's neck over his right shoulder.

'You just want the sugar, don't you? That's all you want,' he says, caressing the bridge of her nose with one hand and pulling down her head, while with the other he feeds her. 'You're awfully greedy. How much sugar could you eat? I don't know why I like you so much!' His eyes begin to water. 'Well, you've got an early start tomorrow. Now mind you behave.' He notices that he is speaking to Contact very much as Nanny speaks to him. This makes him smile. 'Otherwise you'll have to go away and I'll never see you any more. And that's the last lump, you greedy animal,' he says, feeling weak and sentimental. 'Goodnight then,' he says sternly, moving into the sunlit yard.

Contact blows through her nose, and Vere, pleased with that little parting whinny, leaves her and goes indoors to the early bed which has been decreed.

He sleeps lightly and is awake before five o'clock when Mal knocks on his door. His room is full of the dawn. Before switching on his bedside lamp he bends beneath his curtains and looks out of the window. A pale illumination shows the stable archway. The elm tree is a black shape against the sky which is still sprinkled with stars. The air is cold, and a ghostly patch of mist spreads over the field where Contact galloped.

He shivers, draws his curtains, and turning on the light, quickly dresses himself in the thick clothes that have been laid out overnight. Then he tiptoes downstairs in his stockinged feet, puts on his wellingtons and short leather coat, and enters the bright front-hall where the others are slowly congregating.

After a pause the door at the top of the stairs opens and Vere's father appears. He wears breeches and gaiters, neat boots, a black coat of some thick material, and a white stock tied tightly round his neck and fastened with a large gold pin.

'Are you all ready?' he whispers.

His face shines as it always does after shaving, his eyes sparkle, and his presence has an invigorating effect on the children, who stop yawning and rubbing their sleepy faces, and begin to whisper and laugh amongst themselves. Mal comes in with a jug of hot chocolate and some biscuits. Mary opens the front-door. It is grey and cold outside, but much lighter than before. Standing in the porch they drink the frothing chocolate out of steamed glasses, the heat of which warms their hands. Cocks are crowing at the farm, birds are beginning to twitter, the black car is coated with dew.

Leo asks, 'Do you think you'll catch a fox, Dad?'

'We might. It's just the right morning.'

'How can the hounds see? It's so dark.'

'Oh Karen!' scoff the children, still whispering for some

reason. 'It's only early yet. It'll be daylight soon. Besides, they use their noses.'

'There ought to be a good scent today,' their father says, whistling under his breath and seeming to sniff the sharp air.

'What's the time?'

'Shouldn't we go?'

Vere fetches his father's bowler hat, string gloves and riding-crop.

'Your hands are freezing,' his father says as he takes them.

'Are they?'

'What, didn't you know?' He smiles.

'No.' Vere shakes his head.

'Are you excited?'

'Yes.'

'Come on then.'

His father drives the car, lighting a cigarette with difficulty as he does so. Vere, who sits at his side, cannot look at him this morning without feeling tensely hopeful, and it is mainly on account of this that he trembles with excitement and clenches his cold hands. But now his father, Mal – everyone is excited. The meet is to be held in the park of a neighbouring landowner, and soon they pass beneath a stately archway, follow a bumpy road between two lines of chestnut trees, come up with some other cars – horses, bystanders – stop and get out. The sun has risen by this time. Huge sunbeams point into the violet and green sky, and the grass that can be seen through the flat mist gleams like a stretch of water. Sounds hang in the moist atmosphere and are magnified by it – the smart click of horses' hooves on the road, the jingling of bridles, voices, the whimpering of two terriers.

'Where are the hounds, Mal?'

'They will come soon, chéri!'

Several horses are being walked under the trees, and amongst these Vere recognises Contact. He wades towards her through the wet grass.

'Good morning, Kenneth,' he calls to the groom.

'Morning, Master Vere.'

'Hullo, Contact.' The mare blows through her nose as she

did the evening before. 'Hullo there, Contact,' he says, stroking her neck and shoulder, and hurrying to keep up with her swishing steps.

'You come to see the sport?' questions Kenneth in his harsh voice.

'Yes. When will the hounds be here?'

'They'll not be long. Steady, old girl,' he cries as Contact tosses her head.

'Steady, Contact,' Vere repeats.

His father approaches.

'How is she, Kenneth?' he asks, taking a last puff at the stub of his cigarette and spitting out the smoke.

'She's fresh, sir.'

'Doesn't look it.' His father buttons up his coat.

'She's not seen hounds yet.'

'Bring her onto the road.'

'This way – this way, old girl,' says Kenneth, pushing the mare with his shoulder.

'Do you want your gloves, Dad?'

'I've got them. Kenneth, here!'

A little car noses its way along the yellow road and suddenly toots its horn. At the sound Contact tosses her head again and breaks into a springy trot.

'Steady!' says Kenneth roughly, dragging at the mare's bridle.

Contact grows calm, but Vere, who stands at her head while his father mounts, can tell by her breathing and her eyes which show more white than usual that she is in a strained uncertain mood.

'Now you behave, you behave,' he mutters, but because of his own excitement the words seem to carry no weight.

Suddenly he remembers the piece of digestive biscuit he has saved for the mare. He reaches into his pocket – crumbs get under his fingernails – glances at his father who is speaking to Kenneth, and holds out the morsel.

'Contact!' he says in a soft commanding voice.

She lowers her head and begins to nibble the biscuit with her lips.

'There,' he says, 'do you like that? That's your breakfast. Eat it up.'

'What are you doing, Vere?'

He raises his eyes guiltily.

'I was just giving Contact a biscuit.'

His father pulls at the reins, jerking up Contact's head. The biscuit falls from her lips into the grass. She starts sidestepping. 'Don't feed her!' His father frowns as he says this. Then he twists round and calls over his shoulder, 'Why don't you stay with Mal?'

Vere blushes and looks away. Why did his father have to say that, he thinks rebelliously, in such a voice and so loud? What wrong was I doing? All the same he feels he has committed an awful sin. Unpleasant twinges of dread riddle his fresh excitement, weaken and spoil it, and he walks towards Mal apprehensively.

The sun is now shining with cold brilliance. Everything is touched by it – the clearing mist, the trunks of trees, horses, cars. A whip cracks along the road, there is an odd throaty cry, a few deep barks and a whine, and the hounds come into sight. They approach in a compact mass – a single body with many legs and waving tails – the master riding in their midst, whippers-in on either side of them. Admiring cries break from the bystanders. The master, who looks like a hound himself with his wooden face and set expression, begins to greet people in rasping tones and to touch his velvet cap with his riding-crop. The two hunt-servants call the hounds by name and flick at them with their whips. Horsemen answer the master respectfully; everyone seems to be impressed and delighted by his safe arrival; anticipation mounts.

'Nice bit of trouble over there,' Vere overhears somebody say.

He guesses it is his father who is referred to. 'Oh Contact, be good, please be good,' he breathes quickly, half-closing his eyes. Then he looks round. Between the trees, some distance off, he can see the little mare prancing on her slender legs and shaking her head. The master blows a short piercing blast on his hunting-horn. The mare begins to rear up and buck. 'Oh don't, Contact,' Vere implores silently. His father's face is very red and his bowler hat has fallen forward onto his nose. 'Don't make him angry, Contact,' Vere pleads; but he senses that his plea has come too late and of a sudden is filled with despair. Mal touches his arm and he turns away.

The hounds are moving forward. The dozen or so riders jostle after them, then come two cars and the people on foot. Mary, Karen and Leo pass with shouts of glee, their gumboots clumping as they run and their coats flapping open. Kenneth passes with bow-legged steps. The hunt disappears through a gate into a wood and Vere follows slowly with Mal. His father and Contact are nowhere to be seen.

'La chasse, la chasse!' Mal exclaims. 'Don't you love it?'

Vere answers disagreeably, 'There are an awful lot of hounds to catch a fox, aren't there?' Nonplussed, Mal smiles, tightening the corners of her mouth. 'What harm do foxes do?' he continues.

'They kill the chickens!' She looks at him as if she has explained everything. 'I have seen it, when I was young. They do not kill only one chicken. They kill all – in the neck they bite them' – she makes a blood-thirsty sound – 'ten, fifteen chickens!'

'How did you see it?' he asks.

'Well, the fox got into the chicken place and afterwards I went to see.'

'And were they all dead?'

'Mais oui!'

'Was there blood everywhere?'

'Yes – horrible!'

'Is that why foxes are hunted?'

'It is necessary. If not there would be no chickens or eggs.'

'I love chicken and eggs,' says Vere, feeling hungry.

'Moi aussi.'

'I'd love two fried eggs with fried bread and crisp bacon, wouldn't you, Mal – just cooked and hot?'

'Oh don't!' She laughs.

'But I still can't see why they have to have so many hounds,' he says.

They walk for a time without speaking. Then Mal halts and lifts her stick with the rubber ferrule on the end.

'What is that?'

They listen. They are in the wood, at the juncture of several grassy rides. The sun, more golden now, lights up the damp bracken in places and the tangled scrub. A startled jay swoops over their heads, turns silently – its white rump flashing – and vanishes amongst the ornamental trees. A moment later its note of warning is heard, raucous and scolding. A blackbird flies low down one of the rides, sees them, swerves frantically and also begins to scold. An alarmed hush falls over the wood.

'What did you hear?' Vere whispers.

'But there – there!'

A distant bell-like crying, interspersed with some deeper baying and a curious broken yell, comes to their ears.

'Are they killing a fox?'

'Je ne sais pas.'

'But what are they doing?'

'Hunting! Come on! It's thrilling!'

He begins to feel excited again and says to Mal, who is starting to plod down a ride: 'Are you sure that's the right way?'

She stops. 'Why not?'

'We don't know where they went.'

'Then we will find out.'

'Can you hear anything?'

'No.'

'Wait, Mal.'

'No no – come along!' She resumes her heavy walk.

He picks up a stick as he follows her and slashes at tufts of grass, scattering the dewdrops. He thinks of Contact and tries to feel depressed. 'Why is it called cub-hunting?' he asks, although he knows quite well.

'Because it is the cubs they are hunting.'

He wants to say, 'How cruel.' Instead he inquires, 'How will we know when they kill one?'

'We will hear the horn.' She imitates it, puffing out of the side of her mouth.

He smiles crookedly, drops behind, beats the grass with his stick. But all the time he is listening intently and feeling more excited than ever.

Soon after this they emerge from the wood. A bank on which huge pine-trees grow stretches before them, sloping easily down to a lake. Beyond the lake, in a fine position, rises the bare wall of a great shuttered house. A stray hound lollops between the pine-trees and Vere calls eagerly to Mal, running to catch up with her.

'Do you see it? Look – did you see it, Mal?'

'What?'

'The hound! It's gone now.'

'Ssh, we will see the fox.'

'Where?'

'I don't know.' He laughs. 'In a minute.'

Two ducks quack and fly from the lake, splashing loudly.

'Look!' cries Vere. 'There's Contact! Contact and Daddy – look, Mal, look!'

Sunlight flashes on a horse and rider away amongst the pine-trees.

'I can see nothing.'

'They were there!'

'Are you sure?'

'I know it!'

And Contact was cantering! So all may still be well! He squeezes Mal's arm.

'Oh, we'll miss everything – please hurry, Mal!'

He runs ahead over the ground that is covered with pine-needles, hears a noise behind him, slithers to a stop and turns. Mal is lunging forward with her stick. He stares in amazement. Suddenly she tears off her green beret and hurls it towards a pine-tree.

'The fox!' he thinks opening his eyes extremely wide and gazing up the slope.

Fifty yards away, in deep shadow, a small brown object is moving rapidly between the tree-trunks. As soon as he sees it, without knowing why, Vere shouts. The object increases its pace. He shouts again and dashes back to Mal.

'Tally-ho!' she is crying.

'Was it the fox?'

'Tally-ho, tally-ho!' she warbles in her singing voice, nodding her head.

He begins to shout with all the power of his lungs. The fox has gone – he does not look or care for the fox: but he shouts until he is hoarse.

'Mal, Mal!' He can hardly speak. 'They're all at the end here – the hunt and Contact – everything – come quick, Mal, quick!'

'You go!' she insists furiously.

He runs under the pine-trees, attempting to take off his coat as he does so, but he slides and slips on the pine-needles, nearly falls, and allows it to billow and flap. He is unbearably hot and half-crying with the wild excitement that has now taken possession of him. He has seen the fox, he can hear the hounds giving tongue: he has seen Contact and she seemed to be calmly cantering. But not for these reasons alone does he feel so feverishly excited. The real climax is approaching – that is what he feels. Everything, one way or the other, is about to be resolved. This path is the path he has imagined: somewhere along it he will find what he is seeking. And therefore he plunges headlong, so breathless that he seems to have a prickly burr stuck in his throat, under the dark green trees.

He reaches an open space and stops. The bright sun is blinding. He screws up his eyes and looks round. Some riders are crossing a balustraded bridge on his right and galloping up the grassy slope. The horses' hooves throw divots of turf into the air as they pass him. On the other side of the glade in which he is standing an unfenced wood, with neatly-divided areas of bracken and sparse undergrowth, covers the hillside. The hounds are in this wood. He catches a glimpse of them and shouts. Then he starts to run across the glade. Two more horsemen thunder over the bridge. One of them waves at Vere and bellows something. He gazes at the charging horses blankly and scrambles in the nick of time out of their way. He begins to run towards the bridge, realises he is going in the wrong direction, turns about and races back to the last of the pine-trees. A solitary horseman canters over the bridge. It is his father.

'Hullo, Dad!' He waves his arms.

As before, he thinks, if Contact is only cantering, not galloping or bucking, all must be well. And he runs forward a few yards, beside himself with hope and mad joy.

'Dad, Dad!' he screams.

But then he sees that Contact is not exactly cantering. Her head is drawn up and back. She is pawing yet only just touching the ground with her forelegs – which look abnormally long – while her hindlegs are awkwardly gathered underneath her. She seems to falter all the time, as if she wanted but was unable to bound forward. And her neck and flanks are white with hot lather.

'Contact,' he gasps, not understanding.

His father is standing in the stirrups now, dragging with his full weight on the reins. And Contact's head goes up, her neck bulges out, her forelegs leave the ground altogether.

His father's face – he can see it – is purple, contorted. There is a scratch on his jutting chin.

'What's the matter, what's the matter?'

Vere repeats the question several times, not knowing what he is saying.

'Where the hell is Kenneth?' shouts his father.

'Kenneth?'

'Where's Kenneth?'

'I don't know.'

'Go and find him!'

'What?'

'For God's sake go and find him!'

'What's the matter, Dad, what's the matter?'

But he can see what is the matter. He forces himself to move towards Contact, though he feels suddenly sick and paralysed.

'Her mouth is bleeding,' he sobs as if he were still excited.

'Get away from this something horse!'

Vere takes no notice. His father relaxes his hold on the reins for a second in order to obtain a better grip, and Contact lowers her head and stands still. Her mouth is injured and bleeding, her sensitive lips are covered with blood and foam. The steel bit pulls her mouth open. He can see it is full of blood.

'Oh Contact,' he moans.

The mare blows through her nose, which is cut and also bleeding – blows very gently, as if in response.

'Her mouth is bleeding!' he shouts angrily at his father.

'I don't mind if she's bleeding all over!' The reins jerk and Contact rises on her hindlegs.

'Leave her alone!' Vere cries.

'Get out of the way!' shouts his father at the same moment.

'Don't do it – how can you? Leave her alone!' cries Vere in a paroxysm of rage and grief.

'How dare you talk to me like that?' answers his father. 'Go and get Kenneth!' And swearing and muttering he gathers the reins in one hand, raises his ivory-handled riding-crop and whacks it down on Contact's quivering flank.

The mare whinnies. The veins swell in her neck and she careers up the slope, her head tugged savagely to one side.

'How can you?' Vere sobs. 'How can you, how can you?' he repeats over and over again.

He stumbles to his pine-tree and flops onto the ground at its base. 'How can you?' he continues to mumble, sobbing and staring blindly at the bracken opposite. The glade is empty now, the hounds are momentarily quiet. But there, in the bracken, something is moving. He takes a deep jerky breath and focuses his eyes.

A fox is bobbing through the undergrowth. It is not twenty yards away: he can see it distinctly. Now it stops and listens. He can see it has one pad raised. He is reminded of Danny Fox in his favourite 'Little Jack Rabbit'. This fox has the same pointed face he has imagined, and sly expression, big ears, sleek red coat. In spite of himself he feels excited again and stealthily stands up. The fox – but it must be a cub – emerges from the undergrowth and begins to step and jump delicately over the bracken. It reaches the grass ride and pauses, snapping unexpectedly at a fly. Then it leaps over the last clump of bracken, lands without a sound and trots away down the ride.

Ten feet ahead of it a hound appears. Both the fox and the hound stop. For some seconds nothing happens. The hound and the fox face each other without moving on the green sunlit turf beside the bracken. Then the pack of hounds, strangely silent in its approach, bounds into view. The fox turns. Vere tries to shout and runs across the glade. The hounds, with terrible cries and without checking, descend on the fox. One endless high-pitched scream rises above the baying. The fox is caught, torn apart – red limb from limb – tossed in the air, caught again, and worried on the ground by the circle of snarling hounds.

The master rides up, followed by the hunt. He blows a long call on his hunting-horn, then, smiling with pleasure, cheers on and encourages the hounds. The other riders join in and shout congratulations to the master, watching the murderous hounds with evident satisfaction. Beyond the group Vere sees his father, still having trouble with Contact, but laughing now and straightening his stock. He retraces his steps across the glade and finds Mal.

'It is the kill!' she says. 'Why are you so white? What is it, chéri?'

'Nothing, Mal,' he replies.

'Do you want to go back to the car?'

'Yes, please.'

But a man blocks their way. He has a strong nose and thin lips.

'Come with me, nipper,' he says. 'I'll have you blooded.' Mal answers for Vere.

'Not want it?' the man exclaims. 'Aren't you a sport like your father?'

Vere raises his eyes. 'No!' he answers with cold conviction. Never! – he thinks as he walks under the sheltering pine-trees – I will never be like him, never, never, never as long as I live!

EIGHT

WAR

It is the first Sunday in September.

Vere wakes with a horrible start and immediately feels angry.

Leo is standing at the end of his bed, the jacket of his pyjamas open, the white skin of his chest exposed, and his pink shiny face lit by the sun that streams narrowly through the gap in the curtains. 'Wake up, wake up,' he is saying as he swings on the wooden bed-end.

'Go away,' answers Vere, jolted by the creaking motion.

'You go away,' Leo teases.

'Go away, Leo!'

But Leo jumps onto the bed and begins to bounce up and down on the springs. 'It's . . . time . . . for . . . small boys . . . to get up!' he sings out between bounces.

Soon the brothers are fighting. Leo gets the worst of it for Vere fights with fury, taking a certain perverse delight in this violent expression of his careless despair. But his victories are hot and bitter – Leo only laughs and giggles, undismayed by defeat, tirelessly provocative – and the sense of disaster to which he awoke, the anger and the dread, are not assuaged.

'Come on, Leo, it's time to get up. Now stop it.'

But Leo never knows when to stop. He laughs and pushes Vere, who falls backwards onto the bed and hurts his wrist.

'You fool, Leo, you've hurt me, look what you've done!' says Vere, swaying about on the edge of the bed and hugging his wrist. Perhaps it is broken and I will not have to go to school, he thinks. 'Fetch Nanny,' he groans. 'It's really bad. Go and get her, Leo,' he repeats angrily.

Nanny comes and examines the wrist which looks rather normal. 'It's usually Leo who gets hurt about this time,' she says, a reference to the maladies Leo is apt to develop towards the end of the holidays.

Vere pretends not to understand. 'It may look all right. I just can't move it,' he says. Nanny smiles. Angry with Nanny for smiling, and also for comparing him to Leo, he says with a sour laugh, 'Oh, don't worry, I expect it'll get better!' And he walks rudely past Nanny and Leo, enters the bathroom and bangs the door.

He wishes his wrist would suddenly swell and fill with poison. He wants something dramatic and terrible to happen. His mind revolves round catastrophe. He desires the discomfiture of all his foes, and in order to achieve it is more than ready to sicken and nearly die – or in fact die, and so be spared school.

The sunlight is brilliant on the bathroom floor – it warms his bare feet: and outside, on the roof of the stables, the dew is drying, the doves are stretching their wings and cooing, the weathercock is steady. All is sweet and familiar. And he finds it vile, hateful. He leans on the stone bathroom window-sill and imagines with relish some sudden shock – a tremor of the earth, some ruinous explosion – which would disturb the perennial lethargy of the scene he surveys. Only a great exterior tension, he believes, will snap the cords of misery that bind him, only a shattering upheaval free him from the prison of his inescapable rage.

He returns to his room and begins to dress. His fingers tingle under the stress of his emotion, his hair hurts when he combs it, and his skin aches from contact with his clothes. His shirt seems to be made of sandpaper: he feels raw, he positively smarts: and he has a dull pain in his teeth which he discovers he is grinding.

He wonders what is wrong with him. Remembering past pain, he throbs with present anger, future dread. But he shakes himself like a dog and determines to control his ill humour.

At breakfast there is talk of war. The children are full of it and Nanny's anxious expression adds to their excitement. Vere, obsessed by his efforts to keep his temper, says little, but he blushes every time he speaks or is spoken to, and his irritation increases. Towards the end of the meal Nanny asks after his wrist.

Colouring, he repeats stupidly, 'My wrist?'

'Have you forgotten it? It must be better,' Nanny says.

'I thought you couldn't move it,' says Leo, and proceeds to give an amusing account of the incident in the bedroom. 'I should jump out of the window,' he finally suggests. 'Then you'll probably always stay at home.'

'Yes, in a coffin,' adds Karen.

Vere is too angry and miserable to answer. He no longer feels ashamed of his rage; he discards his good intentions. Hatred flares in his heart: hatred for Leo, Karen and even Nanny, self-hatred for having laid himself open to attack. Incapable of giving vent to his fury, speechless as always in face of opposition, he glares round the table. But he cannot meet the intrigued stares that are turned upon him and his hatred melts into self-pity. Excusing himself in a thick voice he leaves the nursery and goes along to say good morning to his mother.

After he has kissed her, for want of something better to say, he mentions the war, but in a cool tone so that it should not appear that he shared the others' excitement. His mother says it is dreadful, and she does not know what they are going to do. Then she says, 'Darling, I found your School List last night. I think you ought to go through it with Nanny.'

Something in his mother's voice makes Vere answer sharply, 'What's a School List?'

'It's no good speaking like that, Vere,' she says, lowering her chin and giving him a reproachful look.

'How was I speaking?'

'In that cross way.'

'I wasn't.' He is startled by his abrupt and disrespectful tone, yet oddly gratified by it. After a pause, looking out of the window, he repeats his question. 'I asked you what a School List is.'

'It's your clothes,' his mother answers shortly. Then she asks, 'Are you very sad about school?'

Taken by surprise he glances at his mother. Her face wears an expression of fearful probing inquiry. Again something in her voice, and in her eyes which she quickly averts – a sort of nervous anticipation – seems to demand brutality; and when she reiterates, 'Are you, darling?' he answers, 'Of course not!' with cruel emphasis.

'And I can't go through the list today,' he adds.

His mother shuffles the newspapers that lie on her white satin eiderdown. 'Now Vere, go and get it finished,' she says. 'I'm only thinking of you, darling.'

He snatches the paper and leaves the room in silence.

A dull precise voice booms along the nursery passage. Nanny and Edith are listening to the wireless.

'We've got to go through this,' Vere says loudly, ignoring Nanny's solemn expression and waving the School List in front of her.

'In a minute, Vere, be quiet now.'

'Mummy says we must.'

'Put it down and be quiet, Vere, there's a good boy.' He throws the paper towards the uncleared breakfast table, but it folds and flutters to the ground. He kicks it, then bends laboriously to pick it up. The blood rushes to his head, there is a singing in his ears, and the voice that issues from the leather-covered wireless seems unbearably loud.

'Nanny, we've got to go through this list,' he shouts.

Nanny rises and turns off the wireless. 'Well, Vere, what is it?' she asks mildly.

'How do I know?' He hands her the crumpled list, regretting the rough way he has spoken.

'Are you well, Vere?'

'Why?'

'You look rather pale.'

He begins to feel sorry for himself. 'I don't know,' he says.

'What is it, Vere?' Nanny asks as she follows him into the passage.

'Nothing, nothing,' he answers. 'Let's go through the beastly list!'

He stalks ahead of Nanny down the passage and enters the darkened spare room at the top of the kitchen stairs. Stumbling over shoes and piles of clothing he reaches the window and pulls the blind. It rattles upwards. The sight that meets his eyes makes him feel weak and he sits abruptly on the lid of his new brown trunk.

'You read out what's written here,' Nanny says, 'and I'll do the checking.'

Vere takes the list and reads. 'One Eton jacket and trousers. Two blue blazers. Three pairs of grey flannel trousers. Two pairs of short trousers, blue . . .'

Nanny kneels on the floor and answers him at intervals. 'Am I allowed to take my tweed coat?' he asks.

'No, just the things on the list.'

'Am I allowed to take my sheath-knife?'

'You know you're not, Vere.'

'Or my yellow tie?'

'What comes next, Vere?'

He reads with heavy sarcasm. 'Five vests and pants . . .'

The angry wasted minutes pass. I will regret this lost time, he thinks; but still the furious thoughts boil within him. Will I always feel the same, he wonders. And because his shocked reactions seem perfectly true, reasonable, and therefore lasting, he sees suddenly a lifetime of anger and hatred stretching before him, and this thought fills him with fresh misery. In order to interrupt the obsessive circle of his feelings he asks Nanny why she was listening to the wireless. She tells him of the threat of war, but he cannot concentrate on what she is saying. He finds himself studying her face with cold detachment, noticing the high hairline, the strong bristling eyebrows, the slightly crooked mouth and the small definite chin. He observes her face as if it belonged to a stranger. But the very barrenness of his response eventually evokes a blunt unhappy ache in his heart.

They continue to sort the clothes. 'Nanny, did you go to school?' he asks.

'Indeed I did.'

'But you lived at home, didn't you?' he challenges her.

'Yes, but it was two miles to school and we had to go in all weathers.'

'How? How did you go?'

'On Shanks's pony. Four miles a day, and often it was cold and wet.'

'I wouldn't mind walking four miles a day.'

'Read out the list, child.'

'One pair of black football boots. Did you like school, Nanny?'

'Well, I wanted to learn and get on.'

'Why?'

She laughs. 'It's natural, and that's how you must think about it, Vere.'

He would like to say, 'But while you were learning and getting on, you lived at home.' Instead, he reads out the last item on the list. He does feel calmer for the conversation, however; and his attempts to picture Nanny as a little girl, trudging to school through snow and sleet, with rosy cheeks and books under her arm, and perhaps an apple in her pocket, divert him. He examines her closely. Did she have those hairs on her chin when she went to school? He cannot imagine her without them. For the first time in the day he smiles.

'There, that's the lot. Oh my poor knees,' she says, rising to her feet with difficulty. Vere wonders if she rose from her school desk in the same way, begging the teacher's pardon for her rheumaticky joints; and once again he smiles. 'All over,' she says as she closes the spare-room door. He remembers that she says 'All over' when she fetches him from the dentist's house in Long Cretton, and is grateful for the tacit admission of his suffering and pain.

'Are you going to church today?' she asks. 'You will be, I expect.'

Wishing to convey his gratitude he thanks her for checking the School List; but the mention of the word 'school' churns up a new storm of dread and despair, and he leaves her in the middle of a sentence and hurries down the front stairs.

His father is sitting at the end of the long hall table. He lowers his paper as Vere approaches and inclines his head to be kissed. Then he says, 'Your hair needs brushing.'

'I know,' Vere answers quickly. 'Are we going to church?' Nowadays he does not address his father by name.

'Do you want to?'

'I don't mind. Are we?' He feels he can only make arrangements with his father.

'I think we'd better. What's the time?'

'Twenty-three minutes and twenty seconds to eleven.' Vere thanks heaven for his watch which he can safely regard and wind. 'What time will we leave?' he asks.

'Ten to eleven. You go and get changed.'

Vere returns to the nursery, enters his bedroom, and begins to bang the cupboard doors, tug at the drawers of the chest and hurl his Sunday outfit onto the bed.

'Now then, now then,' Edith warns him as she passes through the room.

'What are you saying?' he inquires insultingly.

'Don't take that tone with me, Master Vere,' she retorts, accentuating the 'Master Vere'. 'Perhaps school will teach you manners.'

'I didn't hear that, Edith!' Vere shouts. But Edith has closed his door.

He breathes hard as he climbs into his grey flannel suit and half-throttles himself with the yellow tie that he cannot take to school. Out of his window he can see the stable archway, through which Contact will never again walk with nodding head. Out of his other window he can see the roof over which he scrambled to escape from Leo. He busies himself with his clothes. He feels he must rush and hurry, and he fumbles with buttons and breaks a shoelace. He has a dreadful sensation of precious time going to waste – time that he does not know how he would use, except for further hurry, further rush: time that is none-the-less invaluable. He knocks over a photograph of his father on horseback and does not pick it up. His room is in disorder. He marches out of it, slamming the door, and enters the nursery.

Nanny straightens his tie and tells him to pray for peace. On the way downstairs he can hear his mother sending Mary to wash her hands, Leo and Karen arguing about what they will do if war is declared, his father saying angrily to Bella, 'But I left the blessed thing here!' Out-of-doors the car drawn up in the shimmering sunlight seems to share and augment his restless impatience.

The children pile into it and chatter excitedly.

'If there's war, will you have to fight, Daddy?'

'When will we know for certain?'

'I'm going to buy some more cartridges for my gun.'

'Move over, Vere, or I'll fight you.'

'Yes, Vere, move over.'

'But when will we know, Mummy?'

And Vere wonders what he is doing with these people for whom he feels only hatred and distaste.

They arrive at the church and hurry up the gravel path between the gravestones. The bell stops tolling as they tiptoe through the porch and take their places on a bench behind the font. Vere leans forward in an attitude of prayer, but suddenly noticing that Leo is wearing a pair of his socks, he begins to tremble with rage.

The number of a hymn is given out in a reverberating voice, the organ intones the introduction and the congregation rise and sing. Vere compresses his lips until they pulse, tautens every muscle in his body, clenches his fists and holds his breath. Nanny knitted him those green socks. He would like to spring upon Leo and tear them from his feet. He would like to wound and mutilate Leo. He remembers the agile fox, snapping at a fly, neatly leaping over the bracken, and recalls its fate with a shudder. Let Leo be punished in the same way, let everyone be punished – everyone! His vision blurs; he shivers and sweats all over; his anger and his hatred reach a higher pitch of intensity than ever before.

The double doors at the back of the church are noisily opened. People turn. Mr Pole the churchwarden limps up the aisle and exchanges a word with the parson, then limps to his position in the front pew and pretends to sing. The doors remain open. The parson signals to the organist: the music and the voices tail away. A gradual hush descends.

And although he feels sick and ill, and wonders if he is going to faint, Vere's spasm of rage passes.

For a few seconds the hush continues. Shafts of sunlight bar the church, coloured in places by the stained glass of the windows, and a rook caws lazily somewhere outside.

The parson announces that war has been declared and once more silence falls.

The congregation is larger than usual, Vere notices. Again the rook caws. And everyone is surprisingly still. His mother is looking down at her hymn-book, one edge of which she smooths repeatedly with her pointed thumb. His father's face is grave and pensive, and his jaw juts forward as he clamps his front teeth together. The curious silence is prolonged: it grows tense. Leo shifts his weight furtively from one foot to the other: Vere's back begins to ache.

'Let us pray.'

He sits down, feels slightly better, tries to think of the war, but a final wave of choking despair swamps him and bears him helplessly away.

The voice issues from the sunlight – like the voice of God, Vere fancies – 'Let us draw near to Our Lord in this time of our trouble . . .'

How true, how true, Vere suddenly thinks – this time of our trouble – and he grasps at the words as if to save himself.

'Grant us deliverance from the trials and dangers that await us . . .'

Oh Lord, grant that, Vere prays.

'Prepare us for adversity . . .'

Prepare me, Lord, Vere echoes.

'Forgive us our sins . . .'

He is reminded irresistibly of a picture which has floated lately in his mind: of a lagoon, reflecting a clear northern sky, dotted about with boats and ringed by mountains, cut-off, serene and infinitely peaceful. He sees the settlement at the mouth of the lagoon and the arrested drift of evening smoke above it, and he hears the voices that are carried across the water. He loves that picture: he can see it now so plainly. Why now, he wonders. But he dare not question. He closes his eyes and thinks of the rook, Mr Pole, the war – of things that do not concern him. And all the time, like a freed bird, he is cautiously fluttering, a yard from his cage, another yard, afraid to spread his unaccustomed wings, still doubtful of release.

But the war may prevent me going to school, he thinks. Leo nudges him and he stands up. School will come sometime, now or later, he decides. And he smiles at Leo. The hot lump of dread and hatred dissolves in his chest. He opens his hymn-book and inhales the musty air of the church without hindrance. For a second he thinks of the meaningless war and the prayers that fitted his mood so strangely, then he joins in the singing.

NINE

NANNY AND FLORA

Seven days remain to Vere.

He remembers his seven days as he wakes from a long heavy sleep. Then he turns over quickly, curling up, and draws the bedclothes round him. There is a draught beneath his left shoulder. He pulls down the pillow and settles his head into it deeply. He can feel the breeze on his forehead, cool and intermittent, and by opening his right eye a fraction he can see the sunlight and the faint undulation of the curtains. How warm he is, and comfortable. Seven days . . . He dozes and wakes. Seven days . . .

Is a week a long or a short time? He does not know. There are twelve hours in each day and he has only been awake for minutes, yet every second of those minutes has contained a thought, and even a spice of enjoyment. If he can fill his seconds in this way, every second of every minute, every minute of every hour, then a week is an age, a lifetime. He resolves to treasure his seconds, to extract satisfaction intensely from each. That is the secret, he decides . . . And once again he dozes.

But seven days make a week, he thinks, suddenly opening his eyes, and four weeks make a month, and I had a month left just the other day – a month is nothing, nothing! He shivers and turns over in bed, and a moan of regret for the briefness of his seven days escapes him. What can he do in a week, what is worth doing?

His access of despair sharpens his senses. He hears the muted ticking of the postman's pedal-cycle, the sharp rasp of his nailed boots as he dismounts, the sweet ring of his bicycle-bell as it touches the iron of the fire-escape beneath the nursery window. The postman is sorting the letters: Vere imagines he can hear the rustle of paper. And now he is entering the backyard. Bella will receive him in the pantry, Mrs Lark will give him a cup of tea; he will collect the mail, stow it in his canvas satchel, comment on the coming heat of the day; then he will leave the slowly stirring house and bicycle unhurriedly, through the sunlight, back to Long Cretton.

If only I were a postman, Vere thinks with a sigh, as for the third time he turns over in his bed which now seems to him hot and confined. He recalls his anguished and impressive moan and tries to repeat it, but it sounds like the moo of a cow and he is forced to smile.

Still smiling he throws back the covers and extends his bare feet into the sunlight at the bottom of his bed. He wriggles his toes and hopes they will get sunburnt. Perhaps he will not have to go to school. The floor of his room is squared with brightness and the soft breeze billows across his legs. Perhaps on the morning of the day he is to leave Nanny will come and tell him that since he has been so brave he need never go to school. Perhaps he is a prince in disguise and this cruel test is a part of his preparation. He does not feel he is the son of his mother and father, and wonders who knows of his royal descent. His smile spreads: he notices it and stops smiling. However he may dream the fact of the seven days is hard and real. Yet still he cannot quite believe that he is to be sent away from his home, from Nanny and the nursery, from the garden, the high trees – all he knows and loves so dearly.

He jumps up, dresses, and soon it is time for breakfast. One of the budgerigars, belonging to Leo who is staying with his friend Tim, has laid an egg. For some reason this curious occurrence excites Vere.

When breakfast is finished he goes downstairs to the dining-hall. The front-door is open and the flames of the spirit-lamps under the dishes on the sideboard wave and splutter in the gusts of air. His father is standing by the Chinese chest, glancing through his letters, and Vere kisses him good morning, then begins to step in and out of the sunbeams that cut across the oak boards of the floor. Smells of bacon, coffee, clean silver and hair lotion mingle in the room; envelopes are ripped; a maid moves along an upstairs passage and the kitchen door bangs.

Vere, silently, on his rubber-soled sandals, continues to play his intricate game until little by little he becomes aware of the prolonged hush that has fallen. He pauses, interpreting the sounds that are now important – Edith leaving his mother's bedroom, Mrs Lark in her morning tantrum – then looks at his father. As if conscious of the attention focused upon him, although he does not raise his eyes, his father says, 'These are my call-up papers.'

Without understanding what his father means but sensing it is something bad and painful – frightened by this, yet at the same time flattered by the confidence, Vere blushes. He gazes at his father, wishing he could think of something to say. There is a steady silence.

'I've got to report in ten days.' His father speaks in the same surprised and injured voice, staring at the yellowish paper he holds in his large hands. There is another pause and then he raises his eyes.

Leo's birthday, Vere thinks with a start, before the picnic . . . When his father leant on his stick, watching and smiling sadly. Now as he gazes into the blue unhappy eyes he feels an identical sympathy, affection and tenderness. Nothing has changed – nothing ever changes. He is carried back to that other day, that forgotten moment. Yet everything is changed. His dreams and horrible awakening, his illusions and his disillusion – everything is eclipsed by the old and unexpected love that once more wrings his heart. He does not try to speak – he does not know what he should say – but his silence no longer seems to matter. He stands by the black and gold screen and the sunlight of a sudden seems to penetrate and warm his whole being.

His father moves. 'I'll just go and tell Mummy,' he says.

'All right, Dad.'

Vere watches his father mount the stairs in his restrained springing way, then goes through the open front-door. The light makes him narrow his eyes. His unpredictable excitement has increased. He begins to skip over the lawn and to leap from daisy to daisy. He approaches the lilypool with caution, lies full-length on the paving-stones that already burn, and lowers his arm into the glassy water. He opens his hand and moves one finger. He wants a fish to mistake his finger for a worm and to swim close enough for him to catch it. He would not hurt the fish. He would only like to catch one, to examine it, to throw it high above the pool. How it would sparkle in the sun and splash as it fell! How grateful it would be! But perhaps the fall would kill it. Poor little fish!

He is filled with the desire to be bountiful. If he caught a fish he could give it back its freedom. He wishes he could think of something to give his father. But it is not only his father; it is everyone, everything – the pure air, the sky, the trees, the grass – the entire universe on which he suddenly yearns to confer his favour and his love.

His arm in the water looks broken and his finger – is that his finger? – really does resemble a worm. What if one of the ferocious carp were to think as he does? He struggles into a kneeling position and hoists his arm like an anchor. Rivulets bracelet his wrist, flatten and break up, and shapely beads of sunlit water hang on the tips of his brown fingers. He shakes his hand: the fish rise to the glistening shower: he jumps to his feet and the golden fish, with a fearful flashing shimmer, dive downwards and disperse. He runs round the pool, bounds up the steps and hops along the straight paved path.

Why is he happy? He cannot remember. When was he last as gay, lighthearted? Ages, years – a year ago, at least. Why is it, why? The sky was cloudless yesterday, the shadows equally sharp: the grass looked as green, the flowers smelt as sweet, the trees bowed as low and cast as fresh a shade. Today his father got a letter, that is the reason. What did the letter say?

He stops so abruptly that he stubs his toes against the ends of his sandals. What did that letter say, what does it mean? He sees old Harris by the summer-house, chases across and halts behind him.

'Morning, Mr Harris!' he exclaims.

'Master Vere, you give me a start,' Harris answers, leaning on his long-handled edging shears.

'Mr Harris, Daddy got his call-up papers this morning.'

The gardener adjusts his stiff tweed hat with a bent thumb and forefinger. 'Ah, war's a terrible thing, Master Vere,' he says. Diamonds of sunlight, cut by the leaves of the trees, cluster on his rough clothes.

'Why?' Vere asks.

'Your Daddy'll have to leave his home.'

'Like going to school?'

'That's right, Master Vere.'

'He's only got ten days.'

'Yes, that's war.'

'Why do people have to go away?'

'I couldn't say, Master Vere.'

'I've got to go away, Mr Harris.'

'Yes, we'll be missing you round the place.'

'I'll be missing you too.' Vere picks up the weighty shears and starts to clip ineptly. Harris opens a blade of his knife with his strong dark thumb-nail. The leaves rustle overhead and the diamonds glint and rearrange themselves. 'Daddy doesn't want to go away,' Vere says.

'He wouldn't want it.'

'Why do people have to do things they don't want?'

Harris, who has been scraping the bowl of his pipe with the knife, looks up. 'I don't know, Master Vere, that's just how it is.'

'I'll be gone in a week,' Vere says. Then he lays down the shears, thanks Mr Harris and walks away.

Scamp the dog has followed him into the garden. She sits at a distance in her square Sealyham way, regarding him with deep indifference. Once or twice she sniffs, trying to point her rectangular muzzle; then she lowers herself stiffly onto the ground and starts to roll, emitting languorous growls and waving her fat broad paws in the air.

'Oh Scamp,' Vere says mournfully as he kneels beside her. 'Oh Scamp, oh Scamp.'

The startled dog rolls onto its four short legs and stares at Vere resentfully with its black eyes half-hidden by fur.

'Oh Scamp,' Vere says.

The dog growls. Vere tightens his grip of her head. He recalls nervously her evil nature – she once ate her puppies – and the fact that he has always particularly disliked her: and laughing at himself for his foolishness, he releases her suddenly and jumps away.

He continues to laugh and dance about the garden. He feels as if he is tearing off, layer by layer, an accumulation of thick hot clothes. He feels light and free; he fairly tingles with energy; and seeing Mal on the lawn outside the schoolroom windows, taking her regular twelve deep breaths of morning air, he runs towards her, calling 'Quel joli jour, quel joli jour!' and laughing now because she winces at his French. 'Let's have a game of croquet, ma petite,' he cries, and Mal joins in his laughter.

'I will beat you!' she chants as she lumbers indoors.

'Oh ma petite, ma petite,' he repeats, collecting a mallet and the croquet balls, whilst Mal stands in front of the glass adjusting her Robin Hood hat with the long feather.

He rolls the balls through the door, then runs and swings at them wildly. They spin over the smooth lawn, shining in the sun, and he dashes after them, waving his mallet and shouting to Mal to be quick.

She appears on the lawn – her mallet like a toy in her hand – addresses the black ball, sings out 'Vive le sport!' strikes the ball powerfully and pursues it as if nothing has happened.

Vere's eye is splendidly keen today. He seems to sense the track which each ball should follow, the speed and the angle, and he accomplishes feats which make him gasp and giggle. He is so happy. He loves Mal's cries of 'Croquet!' her quick aim and decisive shots, her snatches of song and vast good humour. Sometimes, watching her, he is overcome by that passionate tenderness the large woman is apt to provoke in him. Then he rushes at her fiercely, calls her 'ma petite', seizes her round the waist and tries unsuccessfully to lift her.

'Joue, chéri, joue, joue!'

The balls click and roll cleanly, into the shadow under the trees of the grove, out to the sunlight, through the hoops, against the stick; the heat levels over the lawn; the breeze abates.

'Vere! Where are you? Vere!'

'Mummy?'

Their voices carry and overlap.

'Mummy!' – 'Will you come here a minute, darling?'

He drops his mallet and runs to the far corner of the house, where his mother is closing the iron gate from the backyard. She kisses him and asks him why he did not come to say good morning.

'But Daddy had his papers,' he tries to explain.

'It doesn't matter,' his mother says. 'Darling, something's happened about school.'

For a moment he looks at her uncertainly, then he thinks: I am going to receive my reward. She will tell me I can always stay at home.

'I want you to answer me truthfully, darling,' his mother says.

Yes, he thinks, I will speak the truth, I will explain everything, when she tells me I need never go to school . . . And he gazes at her with his optimistic eyes.

'Tim's caught measles, can you believe it, and Leo's in quarantine.' She pauses, watching him.

'Oh,' he says, and waits for her to continue.

'It's awful, darling, but we couldn't foresee it.'

He does not understand.

'Leo won't be able to go to school until fifteen days after the term's started. I want to know whether you'd mind going alone too much.'

He looks away and immediately says 'No,' in a high polite voice.

'Are you sure, darling?'

'Yes.' He even smiles.

'I'm afraid it's rather a blow, isn't it? You could wait here and go with Leo. Would you like me to try and arrange it?'

'No, really, Mummy.'

'It means you'll be alone for your first fifteen days.'

'Yes.'

'Are you certain you don't mind?'

'Yes,' he repeats politely.

His mother is talking. 'Leo will have to come home today and you won't be able to see him, darling, I'm afraid. I've rung up Flora and she'd love to have you to stay. You could go down this afternoon.'

'Why can't I see Leo?'

'Because he's in quarantine, I've told you.'

'And I've got to go away this afternoon?'

'You haven't got to, darling.'

'To stay with Flora?'

'Well, I thought –'

'And go to school from Flora's?'

'Yes.'

'Does Nanny know?'

'Yes, I've just been talking to her.'

'All right, Mummy.'

'Wouldn't you like to think it over?'

'No,' he replies.

'It can't be helped, darling, these things will happen . . . I'll tell Flora you'll be coming.'

'Thank you, Mummy.'

They separate. He opens the iron gate and closes it behind him. The latch falls with an oiled metallic click. He places his foot on the first rung of the nursery fire-escape, grips the cold metal with his hands and drags himself wearily upwards. When he reaches the window he squeezes through it awkwardly and drops onto the floor. He lands on his heels – there is no spring in him now – hobbles towards the day-nursery door and enters the sunny room.

Nanny is sitting on the low chair by the fireplace, dressing Faith, and she says as soon as she sees him: 'Well, Vere, have you heard the news?'

He nods, shuffles to the sofa and sits down.

'Are you going?' she asks.

Again he nods.

'I told your mother I thought you probably would.'

'But Leo, Nanny . . .' His lip trembles.

'Well,' she says in matter-of-fact tones, 'you'll be on your own and you've always liked that.'

He stares at her with surprise and even resentment. Faith leans sideways, holding out her hand, and he closes her small fingers round his thumb and notes with a certain satisfaction that his lip is once again trembling.

'I'll have to go today,' he says.

'Only to Flora's,' Nanny answers, unclasping Faith's hand. 'And you'll be there a week. And you know how you enjoy being with Flora. You've been begging to stay there ever since she got married.'

He smiles weakly, feeling as he did when he dreamt one night that his little toe was being run over by a steam-roller. He begins to laugh – he cannot stop himself.

'Come along now, pull yourself together, Vere,' Nanny says, rising to her feet.

'But I'm going this afternoon!' he cries.

'Well, be a man about it,' she advises him. 'Are you coming out?'

'No,' he answers, suddenly injured. But the compliant laughter bubbles up inside him and he calls, 'Yes, all right, I'll come, but wait, Nanny, wait!'

He wobbles along the nursery passage, his knees bending in every direction and his arms swinging limply at his sides. He thinks of things like his bones – the bones in his feet which are surely incapable of supporting him, his blood which at any moment may refuse to flow and his flesh that he has heard is mostly water. He feels he is being dissolved by his frightful laughter, but the grisly humour of this thought makes him laugh louder than ever.

From the bottom of the stairs Nanny inquires, 'Have you thought what you'll want to take to Flora's, Vere?'

His laughter ceases. He catches sight of Faith's round eyes and open mouth, giggles painfully, then says 'Oh dear.' As he descends the stairs and follows Nanny towards the backdoor he repeats 'Oh dear' several times, feeling very miserable.

'Have you thought, Vere?'

'How could I?' he replies testily.

Nanny continues unperturbed. 'You'd better take your stout shoes because you're sure to be going farming. And what about your bicycle?'

'I can't take that,' he says. 'It's got a puncture.'

'Well, you can have it mended in Long Cretton.'

'No, I can't.'

'Why not?'

'Well . . . I won't use it if I do take it.'

'How do you know?'

'I just do, Nanny.'

'You take it, Vere, and then you can see.'

They cross the yard and pass through the garden gate. Faith runs under the apple trees, Nanny sits in a cane chair and starts to knit. After a time Vere throws himself onto the warm grass at her feet and says in the gloomiest voice he can muster, 'I suppose Rod might let me have a shot with his gun.'

'I expect he might,' Nanny agrees.

'It belonged to his father,' Vere informs her briefly. Later he says, 'Rod found some cartridges the other day, they're not made any more.'

'You'll have to ask him to let you have a shoot.'

'Shot, Nanny, shot!' he corrects her.

Time passes. Every so often Faith becomes absorbed in a piece of grass or a fallen leaf, picking it up and muttering to herself. Twice, her eyes shining destructively, she makes a dash for the flowerbed and Vere has to run and catch her. But she accepts the restraint with an innocent smile and toddles away as purposeful and unsteady as ever.

'Rod knows where some barn-owls have nested.'

'Does he, Vere?'

'They snore, you know.'

'No, I didn't know that.'

Nanny changes her knitting from one hand to the other.

'Nanny, would you like an apple?'

'Are they ripe yet?'

'The green ones off my special tree are lovely. Shall I get you one?'

'No, Vere, thank you. But get one for yourself.'

He goes over to the squat tree that clings to the crumbling red brick of the garden wall. His eyes follow the outstretched branches and fasten on a plump half-hidden fruit. His mouth waters as he reaches up between the leaves and begins to twist the apple on its stem. At the third twist it falls ripely into his hand. He carries it by the stalk so as not to disturb its subtle yellow-green bloom and runs back to Nanny.

'Look, it hasn't got a mark,' he says, dangling it in front of her.

'It's awfully green, Vere.'

'Oh but it's sweet and juicy, and really hard, Nanny. Are you sure you wouldn't like one?'

'Quite sure, thank you. You enjoy yours.'

His mouth and even his eyes water as he sinks his teeth into the crisp apple, and its sourness makes him catch his breath. Sucking, swallowing and smacking his lips, he munches for some minutes, then, turning the apple in his wet fingers, he questions, 'Nanny?'

'Yes, Vere?' she replies.

He nibbles. 'It doesn't make much difference, about school, does it?' he asks.

'What do you mean?'

'Going alone?'

'Leo went on his own.' He nibbles thoughtfully. 'You must fight your own battles, Vere. You don't always want Leo to look after you.'

'No, I don't,' he says.

'You're quite well able to stand on your own feet. Other boys have to and Leo did, so there's nothing so terrible about it. I'm sure you'll get along fine. Just work hard and persevere and then you'll succeed. And I've no doubt you will, Vere, none at all.'

He smiles with pleasure at her praise.

'Besides,' she adds, 'you've a nice week with Flora before you go.'

He finishes his apple. Nanny returns to her knitting, left elbow tucked against her side, right arm moving, eyes raised now and again for a glance at Faith who runs and tumbles harmlessly amongst the broken shadows.

'Was the apple good, Vere?'

'Yes, it was,' he answers, throwing the core over the garden wall. 'Nanny, I was playing croquet with Mal when Mummy called me and I never told her what had happened.'

'You'd better go and explain then.'

'All right, I will. Goodbye, Nanny.'

'Goodbye, Vere.'

Mal listens approvingly to Vere's edited account of what has taken place, then suggests that they finish their game of croquet. This reminds him of the time that must elapse before his departure, and he hesitates, wishing he could go at once, in his present brave mood. All the same he follows Mal onto the lawn, where the shadows of the white hoops shorten as the sun swings up into the sky, and compared with Drake, plays out the game.

He leaves Mal and enters the house. Upstairs in his bedroom he finds Nanny kneeling on the floor in front of a small open case, and he helps her to pack it with the clothes and objects that suggest only the delightful life he will live at Little Lodge. At length however he forces himself to inquire about his school clothes.

'They can come down on the morning you go,' Nanny says.

'But you'll bring them, won't you?' An anxious tremor passes through him. 'You'll bring them down, won't you? I'll see you again, won't I, Nanny?'

'Yes, Vere. Quarantine or no quarantine, I'll see you off. So don't worry.'

His mother appears on the scene and asks if he would like

to lunch downstairs. Because he has expected to lunch in the nursery and is unable to adjust himself to any fresh change in his precariously balanced plans, his face falls, and his mother, wrongly interpreting his expression, withdraws her invitation, looking away. She tells him she has ordered the car for three o'clock and speaks of the lovely time he will have with Flora. But before she leaves his room she kisses him, placing her hand at the back of his head and touching his cheek with her cool lips.

His father also puts in an appearance. He sympathises, whistles, admires himself in the long glass and asks vague questions, while his nailed boots crunch on the nursery linoleum.

'What on earth's that, old boy?'

'It's a hollow stick.'

'Why are you taking it?'

'I'm going to get Rod to fill it with lead.'

'What for?'

'Hitting people on the head and things.'

'Good God!'

Although his father does not refer to his own departure or anything Vere feels satisfied and relaxed, and is sorry when the unnecessary excuse is made and the boots crunch away down the passage.

Luncheon arrives. Vere has little appetite. As soon as he is able he goes out and says his various goodbyes, shaking old Harris by the hand and mentioning – unwisely – that they will meet at Christmas. Then he hurries up the cinder path. At the nut-hedge he pauses, remembering his purpose, and starts to study the ground with concentration.

It is here – here – that the fire burnt on Leo's birthday last year. That is where his father stood: here the ice-cream was churned: there is the bank on which he lay so happily. He stoops, stroking the green and gold moss. The branches of the nut-trees move and the moss is sprinkled with sunlight. How like that other day – how different! He wanders on.

He follows the drive – right and right again, directing himself as he used to direct Flora when she wheeled him in the bath-chair. Over there in the big field – far over, probably out of sight – he dropped his salt tears amongst the clover and discovered the nest of the friendly hare. He mounts the terrace, disturbing the noisy rooks in the grove, finds his secret path by the summer-house, pushes his way down it and arrives at the overgrown corner where his house once stood. A few dry stakes remain, pieces of plank, a mound of earth, earth with weeds – weeds everywhere. But there is the canvas satchel in which he used to carry provisions and string – there on the ground, rotten, discoloured. How did he come to leave his satchel here? He touches it with his foot. Why did he never build another house? One day he will.

He clambers over the wall and walks to the back-drive. In the dust he can see the tyre-marks of Mr White's motor-bicycle. Beyond is the field where Contact galloped, and his father shot the pigeon in the green and misty wood. A cock crows at the farm. The heat seems to stifle all sounds, to slur them as it does the outlines of buildings and trees. The white doves coo and settle, an instant's trancelike afternoon peace descends, then the bell is jingled from the nursery window.

With his heart full of fond memories Vere climbs the fire-escape for the last time. After bidding Edith and Faith good-bye he picks up his case.

'Can you manage it?' Nanny asks.

'Of course I can.'

He heaves it into the passage and re-enters the nursery.

'There's the car,' says Edith, looking through the window.

'Now Vere,' Nanny instructs him, 'your mother's in her bedroom, so call in and say goodbye to her. And you'll get your bicycle tomorrow. I think that's everything. Well, you'll have to go.'

He glances at Edith. 'Nanny, is my yellow tie packed?' he asks.

'You won't want it, Vere.'

'Yes, I will.'

'It's too late now, I'll send it down.'

'No, Nanny –' he begins to hop about with impatience – 'I must have it, I can't go without it!'

'Oh heavens, child.'

He leads her into the bedroom and whispers tensely, 'I couldn't say goodbye in front of Edith.'

They both laugh and she kisses him. 'So that was it. All right then, child – goodbye, and I'll see you in a week.'

'Goodbye.'

'Give Flora my love.'

'Goodbye, Nanny.'

He carries his case along the passage, dumps it at the top of the front-stairs, and goes and knocks on his mother's bedroom door.

'Vere? Come in.'

He opens the door. The blue blinds are drawn and the room is in semi-darkness. He says guiltily, 'Oh sorry, Mummy, I didn't know you were resting.'

'Come in, darling,' she repeats.

He feels his way round the screen and stands at the foot of his mother's bed. 'Did I wake you up?' he asks.

'No. Are you ready, Vere?'

'Yes, the car's outside.'

'Mary and Karen have been brought home from school . . .'

He waits for his mother to continue, then says, 'Oh, have they?'

'Well, darling . . .' There is an undecided pause. 'Have you said goodbye?'

'Who to?'

'Nanny?'

'Yes.'

The blinds flap softly and unnoticed lights – on a picture-glass, across a mirror – shift and catch the eye. Through the gloom Vere can now distinguish his mother's head, sunk in a high square pillow, and he addresses it in a puzzled voice. 'I think I ought to go.'

'Yes, you must.'

He moves round the bed and kisses his mother. Her cheek is wet! He is so surprised that he starts and steps backwards. Is she crying – is that what it is – is her cheek wet with tears? But why? Why should she be unhappy?

'Goodbye, darling,' she says shakily. 'Let me know how you get on.'

'Yes, Mummy, I will.'

'When you arrive.'

'Of course, Mummy.'

'And darling . . . Goodbye then.'

'Goodbye, Mummy.'

He turns and tiptoes from the room, closing the door quietly behind him.

'Vere!'

'I'm coming!'

He pauses on the landing and takes a few deep breaths, then he picks up his case, relieved to be able to exercise his taut muscles, swings it lightly down the stairs and goes with Mary and Karen to say goodbye to Mrs Lark, Ethel and Bella. Mal and his father are waiting in the front-hall when he returns.

'Goodbye, chéri, and good luck!'

'Goodbye, Mal.' He kisses her.

'Goodbye, old boy. Look after yourself.'

He kisses his father and looks freely into his eyes. 'You'll be leaving, Dad, in ten days, won't you?'

'Yes, we're in the same boat.' His father smiles gently.

'Goodbye, Dad.'

'Goodbye, monkey.'

They go out. Vere gets into the car, Mary and Karen jump on the running board.

'Gosh, I envy you – going to Flora's!'

Albert starts the engine.

'Tell me about the budgies' egg!' Vere suddenly calls.

'Ready, Master Vere?'

'Let me know about the budgies – whether the egg hatches, won't you?'

The car moves. Mary and Karen run beside it. Vere puts his head out of the window.

'You won't forget, Karen!' he shouts. 'Goodbye, Mal! Goodbye, Dad, goodbye!'

Scamp chases the car, barking. The cries of the girls grow fainter. The car gathers speed. Scamp is out-distanced. With a pang Vere sees her stop, sit down and heedlessly scratch herself. Then, intent on the happy life that is no longer his, he sees his father turn and re-enter the house, Mal and the girls make for the croquet lawn. The car dips down the incline. Only the upper windows of the house are visible, only the stone-tiled roof and the sky, only the arching green trees of the drive . . . But Vere continues to peer in the direction of the scene he can no longer see.

When the car stops at Little Lodge and Albert says, 'A week from now and bright and early!' Vere answers, 'That's it, Albert,' in a passably brisk voice.

After the car has backed down the lane he opens the gate in the wire-meshed fence and drags his case which again seems heavy up the short dusty path to the porch. The front-door is open and he enters and calls, 'Flora?'

'Is that you, Vere? I'm out at the back.'

He follows the passage with its sharp left and right turns and emerges into the sudden light of the glass-roofed shelter behind the bungalow. Flora comes out of the coal-shed. She has a shovel in her hand and her cheek is smudged, and she smoothes her hair when she sees him and smudges her forehead.

'Oh Flora,' he laughs.

'Did you shut the front gate, sweetheart? Chinky'll be off otherwise.'

He laughs again, as always pleased by the ceaseless Little Lodge activity, runs through the house, sees the mongrel Pekingese disappearing down the lane, pursues it and picks it up. Flora is in the kitchen which also serves as living- and dining-room when he returns, and he sits on the good end of the sofa and talks to her while she riddles the oddly-shaped range with its ovens and hobs. They speak of Chinky, of Rod who is harvesting, of the picnic tea they must prepare and take out to him, of the things they must first go and buy in Long Cretton. They do not speak of the circumstances of Vere's arrival. The room is shaded by the trees of the lane and the windows are open. On the high mantelshelf stand a clock with a loud tick, a photograph of Flora's wedding in a chromium frame, a Toby jug filled with used newspaper spills. Flora bustles away with the coal-scuttle. Vere chases after her with the shovel. They laugh; he unpacks his case and looks for Chinky's lead.

He calls to Flora when he finds it and she joins him in the porch, her scrubbed face shining and a basket with money in the bottom over her bare freckled arm. They lock the door and hide the key under the mat, forgetting the open windows, then set out for Cretton, Flora with her quick walk – toes a little turned in, knees a little bent – Vere pulled along by the dog.

'What a thing about Leo, sweetheart, isn't it?' says Flora soon.

'Yes, I know,' Vere answers, and he tries to tell how everything has happened.

Talking, interrupting each other, sometimes laughing, full of relief and information, they walk in the centre of the tarmac road which blisters darkly in the sun.

But just before they reach the High Street Flora asks, 'Did you mind leaving, sweetheart?'

Oh Flora, why that question, he thinks. He looks straight ahead of him and does not reply. He cannot lie to Flora, cannot satisfy the demand for a brave answer the question has always contained: and he has learnt not to tell the unwanted truth. He meets Flora's eyes reproachfully. And they hold no demand, no pressure at all, no threat.

'A bit,' he says, and the admission as if by magic seems to remove an habitual burden from his shoulders.

'Yes, you would,' says Flora simply.

He longs to tell her more, really to tell her everything, and he recalls an impression he has attempted to blot out, of the group of figures which dispersed unfeelingly as he was being driven away by Albert. Breathing shortly, partly from distress, partly because of his daring desire to speak the whole and exact truth, he says, 'Mary and Karen went to play croquet with Mal when I was leaving.'

'Did they?' she comments, and her quiet continuing interest is like attention to his hurt – to all his hurts – soothing at last and healing too.

'Of course they got the afternoon off from school because of me.' His generosity surprises him. 'But I did mind awfully all the same,' he adds, smiling suddenly and feeling brilliantly happy.

They turn the corner into the High Street.

He asks her what she has to do. She fixes her eyes on some faraway object as she tells him; this, and that, and oh yes, the next thing. Then they exchange a look – one of those looks ending in laughter – and he goes and buys two ice-cream cornets. He licks one of them, meanders about contentedly, finds Flora and presents her with the other.

'Oh Vere, you shouldn't have,' she says.

'But Flora, you love ices.'

'I have got a sweet tooth.'

'Yes, you have,' he says.

They return to Little Lodge and prepare the picnic tea. Then they sally forth again, down the lane, over the meadows, up to the field where the yellow sheaves of corn are being gathered and stooked. Rod comes to meet them. They collect some sheaves and sit in the sunlight, eating their new-bread sandwiches, fresh doughnuts and cream-buns, and drinking their warm sweet tea out of individual bottles. Rod, his heavy forearms thatched with golden hair, uses the whole of his hand to grip his sandwiches and takes careful tearing mouthfuls. Vere copies him.

When tea is finished Rod and the other men rise to their feet, and roughly brushing off crumbs and calling to one another, resume their work. Vere carries the sheaf of corn on which he has been sitting and leans it against one of the nearby stooks. Flora shows him how to make a stook of his own and he starts to gather the sheaves, to stumble into line with them and to settle them on the ground in the correct fashion, shaking their heads together so that they hold and stand firmly. The stubble scratches his ankles, he itches all over and sweats, but he races backwards and forwards, fetching the sheaves he is scarcely able to lift.

Mr Durrant the farmer appears in the field, wearing breeches and gaiters and kicking out his short bowed legs when he walks. He thanks Flora and Vere for their help and invites them to come to tea one day.

'Bring Rodney up,' he calls, strutting away with his hands clasped over the protruding flap in the tail of his coat.

Vere stooks the last rustling sheaves in his line and looks round. Flora is speaking to Rod, who pushes back his sharp-peaked balloon-like cap and frees his spiky upstanding forelock. The other men are moving towards an adjacent field, where the horse-drawn reaper clatters and turns. Some of them pause in the gateway and swig at their half-empty bottles of tea: one shouts and chases a rabbit.

Vere signals eagerly and runs ahead. Evening shadows are beginning to slant and sprawl, but the sun is still strong, he notes, determining to work for hours, until it is dark, even by moonlight. Rod and Flora join him. They gather and stook in unison, silently smiling at each other from time to time, while the reaper circles and slices the wedge of standing corn in the centre of the field, the sun slowly sinks and the sky changes colour.

But now Vere stops to watch the rabbits that bounce clumsily over the stubble, works for a spell, then stops to watch again. The insides of his arms and wrists are badly scratched. He tries to lift a final prickly sheaf, fails, sits down on it instead, and surveys the indistinct scene.

'We've done enough, sweetheart, come along home,' says Flora.

'Have we?' He smiles at her wavering outline, then shuts his eyes tightly and shakes his head. 'Flora, pull me up.'

He says goodnight to Rod.

'You ought to get paid for what you've done,' Rod observes in his quiet amused voice. 'We'll have to see about that. Night-night, Vere.'

Flora carries the basket, Vere swings a bottle in either hand. They wander between the stooks, sometimes separating, sometimes together. When they reach the stile they stop and look back. The reaper clatters across the red-gold fields, men faintly shout, but these sounds mingle with the nearer hum of swarming midges and the buzzing of flies.

'You're dropping, sweetheart, come along, come along.'

They trail up the lane and let themselves into the house. Vere enters his small room and puts on his pyjamas. Flora brings him a glass of milk. He sits on the edge of his hard mattress and drinks without opening his eyes. The sounds that he noticed when he stood by the stile still ring in his ears. Flora lifts his aching legs into the bed. She kisses him and draws the curtains. He does not hear her close his door.

After that moment at the top of the High Street when he told Flora how much he minded leaving his home, it never occurs to Vere to wonder if he is happy. The life that he leads absorbs and satisfies him; and because it is complete, because there is nothing false or discordant about it, he does not feel the need to withdraw or dissociate himself. The short days pass in a haze of activity, the nights in dreamless and unnoticed sleep.

These days at Little Lodge assume a pattern. Flora does not call him in the mornings. Rod has already left for work by the time he gets up and he breakfasts alone in the airy living-room. Then he helps with the housework and bicycles into Cretton to buy things for Flora. Rod returns for the midday meal. The afternoons and evenings they spend together in the fields.

On the few occasions that Vere is able to sit down and rest his stiff limbs during the days, he is overwhelmed by a powerful circulating drowsiness he cannot resist. One morning he nods at the breakfast table. This racking but pleasant tiredness surprises him, for he grows capable of longer and longer periods of heavy work, and by the third day is not more tired in the evening than he was when he awoke.

Although Vere accepts his life with Flora and Rod unthinkingly, certain aspects of it he knows that he loves in particular: Flora's forgetfulness, for instance, and the extra work this causes her, or the conscientious way in which Rod tackles the simplest task, or their harvesting, their picnics, the exhausted walks home. He loves the breezes that steal through the ever-open doors and windows of Little Lodge, the smell of frying sausages that makes the hour before luncheon a torment, the transparent red jelly that sets in the shade of the porch: and then the salt that is always damp, bread which crackles when it is cut, clear and icy water from the well – all these things Vere particularly loves. But perhaps without knowing it what he loves most of all is the deep sense of rhythm that these halcyon days engender. The tributaries of his hopes, fears, sorrows and joys are at last united, and the fulfilled stream flows peacefully, smoothly, irresistibly forwards.

On the sixth day of his stay there is a change in routine. No picnic tea is prepared, and at four o'clock Flora and Vere leave the harvesters and return to Little Lodge. They wash and tidy, then set out for Park Farm where Mr Durrant lives with his sister.

The weather has continued perfect and this afternoon it is hotter than ever. They go by the road. Flora wears her crumpled white linen hat and carries a branch of elder against the flies. Vere walks beside the burnt grass of the verge, reminded of what awaits him on the following day and feeling for the first time restless, apprehensive and occasionally sad.

Arriving at Park Farm they ring the bell in the porch that is encrusted with ivy. Miss Durrant comes to the door and immediately leads them away to look at her aviary, her bees, her garden, her geese, and her brother's horses and greyhounds. Vere cannot concentrate on these wonders and is glad when they meet Rod and Mr Durrant, enter the house and sit down to tea in the low oak-panelled dining-room.

When the many plates on the thick oak table have been cleared, Rod leans back in his chair and says smilingly, as if he expected everyone to laugh, 'Are you going to give Vere and me a treat, Mr Durrant, and let us see your racers now?'

The farmer grins and gets up, and without apparently answering Rod's mysterious question, pulls out his watch, holds it in the hollow of his hand, studies it for a moment, then says, 'Right-ho, Rodney, yes, that's the time.'

'But where are we going?' Vere whispers to Rod, as they follow Mr Durrant out of doors.

'You wait and see.'

They approach a black-and-white striped shed that stands in a grass field at the side of the house. A tremendous burbling, cooing, fluttering noise seems to rock this raised shed. In order to make himself heard above it Mr Durrant shouts, 'Ever seen any racing pigeons before, Vere?'

'No!' Vere shakes his head.

'These are my beauties! Time for their fly-round! You stay with Rodney!'

He mounts the wooden steps and sidles through the door into the loft, closing it quickly behind him. The burbling increases. Suddenly a hatch in the side of the loft swings open. A cloud of pigeons, some brown, some nearly white, some grey, with their pale underwings and jewelled throats – a feathery swift cloud issues from the hatch, and swooping low over the field, begins to rise steeply into the sky.

A shiver runs down Vere's spine. The pigeons space out and lift magically above the tops of the elm trees. Turning, they begin to describe huge high circles round the farm. A white one is leading, a dappled one succeeds it, then a grey one, then another white. Dipping and soaring, each pigeon flying wildly, rapturously, they disappear from view behind the roof of the house.

'What did you think of that?' Rod asks.

'Oh they're lovely!' Vere cries, catching some of the soft feathers that swing in the still air.

Mr Durrant opens the door of the loft and looks upwards, puckering his thin lips. He asks Rod to fetch some water, then turns to Vere.

'They'll be over Cretton by now,' he says, jerking his head towards the reappearing pigeons.

'Already?' Vere calls. 'But what are they going to do?'

'They'll be back shortly.'

'Here?'

'That's right.'

Vere moves into the field and sits down. He hears a bucket clink and the voices of Rod and Mr Durrant, but although the sun makes him sneeze and blink, he cannot tear his eyes from the speedy circling birds. Mr Durrant warns him to sit quietly, as the pigeons will soon be starting to home, and he and Rod position themselves beside the shed. Round and round fly the pigeons, in tighter and tighter circles, then with one accord they dive and skim across the field. The air rushes in Vere's face: he swivels, laughing, and sees the pigeons lift again over the elm trees. But now they are flying in a different way, stretching their long wings fully, allowing them to curve and droop, tumbling suddenly and twisting, then climbing almost vertically into the sky. They near the loft, playfully sheer away. The flock scatters. Pairs of pigeons rise one above the other, drop like stones, once more sweep up.

'Oh, oh!' cries Vere.

The pigeons begin to settle. Two are left, a white one and a brown. Sometimes their wings beat together as they soar and circle, sometimes the sun catches their pale feathers or colourful necks. High into the blue sky mount the two pigeons, then with a shudder they descend, flap hastily, alight. They enter the loft and the hatch is closed.

Vere leaves Park Farm, after thanking Mr Durrant and his sister warmly, in a changed mood. Before going to bed that evening he eats a cream-bun and drinks a glass of milk in the living-room. Flora sits at the other side of the table, Rod on the sofa with his hands placed together and gripped between his knees.

'Do you remember the cream-bun I once ate, Flora,' Vere says, 'the day my tooth fell out?'

'Do you remember the bee-sting?' She laughs and covers her face.

'Do you remember when Nanny caught me smoking?' Chinky lies in the passage, nose in a patch of rosy sunlight that streams through the open front-door. Faint sounds from Cretton, of a bus on the hill and the town clock, accentuate the busy quiet surrounding the bungalow.

'Do you remember that nurse when I was ill?'

Midges congregate outside the windows and juggle up and down.

'And the oranges with sugar?'

'And Mr Bruise?'

'What happened when you were caught smoking?' asks Rod, who is never tired of hearing these stories.

Vere and Flora reminisce, their eyes shining retrospectively, their lingering laughter filling the silences, while Rod tilts his head and listens. Now and again Vere glances about him, imprinting the scene on his memory, treasuring each of the slowly-ticking minutes that seem to contain the whole essence of his stay at Little Lodge – all the love and the joy, all the friendship, all the freedom.

'Look at the time, sweetheart.'

'A little longer, Flora.'

'Come again, Vere.'

'I wish I lived here.'

'Come in the winter, then we'll take the ferret out.'

'We never shot with your father's gun.'

'Christmastime we will.'

'And you never showed me the owls.'

'They've flown now.'

'Have they?' says Flora, staring out of the window.

'There'll be some more next year.'

'Bedtime, sweetheart.'

The atmosphere alters. Vere imagines he can see his essential joy, so fragile, so marvellously strong, flit through the sunlit doorway. Perhaps because they have spoken of a future he cannot assume, of omissions now beyond remedy; perhaps because he became aware of it; or perhaps simply because of the relentless advance of life – that sweet mood passes.

Attempting to recall it, he says, standing up, 'Do you remember Leo's birthday?'

'You did enjoy that, didn't you?'

'Yes.' But then he thinks of his old criterion of happiness. 'I liked being here more,' he says.

He shakes Rod by the hand, bidding him goodbye, and goes to get ready for bed.

Everything is clear, everything complete. Even the passing of his gently joyous mood has left him with a sense of rectitude and peace. But now his desire for clarity turns on his arrangements for the following day, and when Flora comes to say goodnight to him he questions her closely. She explains that Nanny is arriving at nine o'clock in the morning with his school clothes and that therefore he had better breakfast in bed.

'Then you'll only have to dress the once.'

He asks what time he will have to go.

'Round half-past nine,' she tells him. And he will motor all day with Albert, picnicking on the road, and arrive at school about four o'clock.

'How will Nanny get home?' he asks.

'She'll take the bus.'

He kisses Flora goodnight and composes himself for sleep. Soon his interior flutterings become suspended, detached. The next thing he knows is that his curtains are being drawn and the early sunshine is flooding his room.

The moment Vere wakes he recollects the significance of Flora's action and his heart sinks. But something good inside him, something sound and solid, seems to act like a shield: and this sudden sinking of his heart, this awful descending feeling of dread and uneasy excitement, is miraculously arrested.

Flora brings him his breakfast tray and he eats hungrily his boiled egg, crisp toast, butter and jellied marmalade. Every so often he thinks of what is going to happen, stirring up feelings of dread and testing the strength of his extraordinary shield. As one after another these feelings are withstood and even repulsed, his uncertain spirits improve.

As soon as he has finished his breakfast he jumps out of bed and begins to run about the bungalow in his pyjamas. It is a fine September morning. The sun shines on the dewy grass, from which rises a thin low mist. Fresh breezes move the curtains at the sides of open windows, and the tiles in the passage are clouded in places with moisture. Vere is chasing Chinky towards the front-door, shouting and laughing, when he first catches sight of the big black car parked in the lane. He stops dead, and a great shaftlike shiver of fear plunges in the direction of his stomach. But once again his inner shield preserves him. The shiver seems to bounce off it and to shatter into harmless fragments. Shaken but unscathed, he calls to Flora and approaches the porch.

When Nanny sees him she says, 'Go in, Vere, go in for any sake – you'll freeze to death, child, without anything on.'

He laughs delightedly, tells her how tough he has become, and leads her into the living-room, where she and Flora embrace awkwardly. Then he takes his case from Albert, fetches Nanny, and with her assistance begins to dress.

For the last week he has worn only sandals, shorts and open-necked shirts, and the long black trousers he now climbs into, the socks and lacing shoes he puts on, and the stiff shirt that fastens with a stud – these unnatural clothes oppress him. But he has so much to say to Nanny that he scarcely notices what he is doing until the time comes for him to fix his starched Eton collar.

'Have I got to wear that?' he exclaims.

'Of course, Vere,' Nanny answers.

Together they tug and pull, bruising their fingertips, and eventually manage to attach the collar to the studs. Nanny slips on his black waistcoat and short jacket, and he goes to the mirror to brush his hair. And his heart sinks with new and horrible violence. His shield seems to bend beneath the blow. He cannot believe it will withstand this sickening onslaught, yet out of a curious perversity he continues to stare at his dreadful reflection, to look out of the window at the waiting car, and to strengthen the very forces he is trying to overcome. But his valiant shield holds. His horror and his fear retreat.

Nanny, who has been fetching his toothbrush, re-enters his room and regards him oddly. He is not surprised. He feels pale and ill, and wonders what would happen if his heart should sink again in such a way. For his interior armour now seems to disintegrate. In its place – in place of his protective shield – is something large and battered, raw, swollen and extremely sensitive.

Flora comes and asks how they are getting on, admires Vere's appearance and says she has coffee ready in the kitchen.

Before leaving his bedroom Vere looks round and says, 'The first night, Nanny, I went to sleep so quickly I didn't hear Flora close my door.'

'You must have been tired,' Nanny observes.

'That was when we started harvesting. I soon got used to it.'

'Well, it's hard work.'

'Feel my muscle.' He crooks his arm.

She squeezes it and says, 'Good gracious me.'

'You can't feel it properly because of these clothes.'

'Come along, Vere, let's go and have our coffee.'

They move into the living-room which Flora has tidied, and sit down. Flora pours the coffee out of the saucepan into three yellow cups, and Nanny says, after rummaging in her bag, 'While I remember, Vere, here are letters from your mother and father.'

He opens his mother's first. She encloses a pound note, which pleases him, and writes on thin paper in a small delicate hand, 'Darling, here is a little something for you to spend at school! Nobody's caught measles yet, luckily. I hope you have liked being at Flora's. I will bring Leo to school in two weeks, so it won't be long before I see you. This term is quite short and then it will be Christmas. Don't be too unhappy, darling. Fond love, Mummy.'

His father encloses two pounds, unevenly folded, and writes on one side of a double sheet of crested paper: 'Dear old boy, I've got to go off in a few days so probably feel a bit like you. No news here. The horses are being sold tomorrow. Most of the men have got to go into the army. I wonder what'll become of us all. Here's a bit of cash. Must close now – Daddy.'

Vere puts away the three pounds, lifts his cup of coffee which Flora has placed on the floor beside him, and takes a sip. The hot liquid seems to scald that sensitive lump in his diaphragm. He chokes, spilling a few drops of coffee, reaches for his handkerchief, remembers it is not in its usual pocket and begins to say, 'How silly –' But noticing Nanny's odd, watchful and almost stern expression, and Flora's wide tender look, he stops and rubs at the spots on his knee in silence.

'We had tea with the Durrants yesterday,' says Flora.

'Oh yes?' Nanny raises her cup, left hand spread beneath it.

'Vere went with Rod to see Mr Durrant's pigeons.'

'Did you, Vere?'

'Yes. There were two . . .' He has so much to tell Nanny. The thought of it overwhelms him. He says, 'They were lovely,' and is thankful because of an unruly depth in his voice, a breathless quality he is afraid may betray him, that he attempted to say no more.

For a little longer they talk in polite strained tones. Then Nanny looks at the clock on the high mantelshelf and says, 'Well, Vere, you've a good drive ahead of you. I suppose you'd better be going.' And she stares at him solemnly through her spectacles.

He wishes he could instantly depart, but Nanny has risen and begun to unfold a black overcoat which has lain across the back of the sofa.

'Whose is that?' he asks, knowing quite well but wanting to say something light and possibly funny.

'It's yours, Vere. I'll help you on with it,' Nanny replies seriously.

'I won't need it,' he says.

'Yes, you will – it's sharp out.'

'But I was in my pyjamas! . . .' The memory of that happy time in his pyjamas hurts him. He adds savagely, 'And look at all I've got on now!'

Flora says, 'But sweetheart, the front of the car's open and Albert's wearing a heavy coat.'

He turns and sticks out his arms behind him. While Nanny helps him into the coat he studies a corner of the ceiling. Then he says, 'I'm absolutely boiling as it is!' and looks round with a smile that trembles, still trying to make light of his impossible situation. But both Nanny and Flora now regard him solemnly and remain silent, so he returns to his study of the beamed ceiling and says in a deep jerky voice, 'The coat goes under my collar, Nanny.'

'Vere, I don't think it does,' Nanny answers.

He waits a second before saying, 'I've seen Leo with it under his collar a hundred times.'

'Are you sure, sweetheart?'

'Yes!'

'Well, we'll try it, Vere.'

He knows he is not believed. The insupportability of this further disagreement causes the sensitive lump inside him to swell. As Nanny struggles with the collar which already covers his waistcoat and jacket, and the tightness round his neck increases, the cruel pressure seems to bear directly on that lump, enlarging it moment by moment and paining him more and more. Yet he does not protest. He is certain he is right. And to give way over the collar would be to give way completely, to everything.

'There you are, Vere,' Nanny says finally.

He turns. Suddenly, because the collar is too tight, because he realises he has been wrong, because of the fond earnest glances that he meets, and the expectant hush, and all that has gone before, he is overpowered by violent anger, antagonism and resentment. He starts to say something. Burning damaging words rise to his lips. He makes a single unintelligible sound, then everything changes. His rage and hatred leave him. The whole edifice of conflict, control, containment of his grief, topples to the ground.

'I can't breathe,' he says.

'It's all right, child, it's all right now,' Nanny says quickly, removing the coat from beneath his collar.

'I can't go,' he says.

'You must, Vere.'

'I can't, I can't!' He clings to her hands.

'Say goodbye to Flora.'

Now it is Flora he clings to. He feels her lips on his face, sees her blue eyes. Nothing is distinct.

'Goodbye, my sweetheart.'

'Oh Flora, I can't.'

He seizes her jersey and her hands. Then it is Nanny he is kissing and holding.

'Don't!' he cries, meaning, Don't make me.

'Yes, child, you must.'

There are her spectacles above him and her straight eyes. He cannot move, speak, see or feel. He is robbed of every sense by his paralysing sobs. And he does not care about school. All he minds is being parted from Nanny and Flora.

'I can't, I can't . . .'

He does not know where he is, what he is doing. There is Chinky – the tiles in the passage – the porch.

'I can't!' he cries.

Please, Vere . . . Sweetheart . . . Child . . .

'No, Nanny . . . No, no, Flora!'

Albert helps him into the car. Nanny and Flora stand by the gate in the wire fence.

'I'm so sorry,' he tries to say.

'Be a good boy, Vere . . . Be good, won't you?' Nanny repeats.

He nods. Everything becomes blurred: Nanny, Flora, Chinky chasing the car, Little Lodge, a curtain blowing through an open window, the trees in the lane, the bright morning sunlight. He lowers his head and abandons himself to his sobs.

Very slowly, after a stretch of time which he cannot estimate, Vere pulls his handkerchief out of its new pocket. He wipes his eyes that are damp and sandy, and his face, hands and overcoat that are wet. Then he lays his hands with the fingers splayed on his knees to dry, and attempts to concentrate on the spasmodic movements of the needles of the black dials set into the dashboard. But he believes that he feels too miserable, too lethargic: therefore he sits hunched, blows out his hot swollen lips, allows his vision to become fixed and obscured. And again time passes.

'Sixty-five miles an hour!' states Albert unexpectedly.

'Really?' says Vere, looking out of the window.

Albert says no more, yet his single comment and the start of latent interest it has aroused force Vere to admit to himself that for some little while he has felt neither miserable nor lethargic, but strangely tense and excited.

He tries not to think of his strange excitement and continues to look about him. Birds swerve out of the thickset hedges, horses canter in a misty field. The car halts and a flock of sheep scuttles by. Vere returns the salute of the grave shepherd, watches his active dog, savours the warm smell of the animals, observes their yellow eyes.

And suddenly it seems to him that the world is not as it was. He cannot postpone realisation any longer: each object of the once more moving scene deepens his ache of wonder and of joy. For everything is changed. He thinks of Nanny and of Flora, then of sheep, shepherd, trees and pale blue sky, of all he sees, all he has known and may ever know – and he is not afraid.

'All right now?' Albert asks.

'All right,' Vere answers.

DAI HOUYING

STONES OF THE WALL

The aftermath of the Cultural Revolution in China appeared to mark the end of a reign of terror and suspicion. But in China's universities, which form the backdrop to the novel, and where many of the struggles of the Revolution took place, students had to face a new and extraordinary situation.

STONES OF THE WALL is about a group of people trying to rebuild their lives into a new and uncertain future. The first major novel to emerge from contemporary China, it is both a story of individuals and of mass politics, a rare glimpse behind the inscrutable face of the Orient.

'The first major novel from China to be published in thirty years'

Loyd Grossman in The Sunday Times

'I trust her judgement as well as admire her work'

D. A. N. Jones in The London Review of Books

'Ambitious and brave . . . a powerful immediacy . . . a fascinating and touchingly human novel'

Teresa McLean in The Tablet

sceptre

PATRICE CHAPLIN

ALBANY PARK

Patrice and Beryl, teenagers in the 1950s, live in Albany Park, a South London suburb. Life is full of make-up, boys and trad jazz in Soho; dreams are all of Hollywood. En route to this better life, they hitch-hike to Spain, where they meet the charismatic writer, José Tarres. For Patrice Chaplin it is a meeting which will mark the end of a friendship and the beginning of a lifetime's obsession.

Written in a refreshingly engaging and direct style, ALBANY PARK is a glorious evocation of teenage life in the 1950s.

'Full of freshness, incident and humour'

The Times

'. . . Perfectly pitched and painfully funny . . . a very immediate piece of writing in which perspectives edge into the narrative like coming shadows . . . Chaplin is a true original'

New Society

'The best offbeat evocation of a country since Laurie Lee's'

Daily Mail

sceptre

GORDON LISH

PERU

A newsflash about an atrocity triggers off an odd confession from middle-aged, Manhattan-living Gordon. He recalls how he committed an act of hideous violence as a child. Everything is recounted in microscopic, second-by-second detail. Yet did it really happen or 'are words not the point?'

'Every novel is new. This one may be unique'
The Washington Post

'Its mesmeric voice requires, and rewards, a close reading'
Time

'An amazing book . . . obsessive and obsessions remain fascinating'
Stephen Dobyns in The New York Times

'A stunner . . . evokes with unsettling vividness the darker feelings of childhood . . . Haunting and disturbing . . . an absolute original'
Anne Tyler, author of THE ACCIDENTAL TOURIST

sceptre

JEREMY COOPER

RUTH

A searingly evocative portrait of a young artist living and working in rural Somerset, and of her struggle to overcome a debilitating mental illness. RUTH is as compassionate as it is memorable.

'A first novel . . . and one of the year's best'

The Observer

'Written in a calm and clear style, with excellent detail . . . reading it is to be reminded what a noble activity the craft of novel writing still is'

The London Standard

'RUTH is a very painful book to read . . . What is impressive is not just the conviction with which he paints the world as seen by Ruth, but the fact that he makes no attempt to manipulate our emotions. It is a remarkably controlled novel'

John Nicholson in The Times

'Jeremy Cooper has produced the best first novel that I have read in a long time'

Harriet Waugh in
The London Illustrated News

JANICE ELLIOTT

THE ITALIAN LESSON

The Castello of San Salvatore is an exclusive and enchanted holiday place set in the hills above Florence and far removed from the dangerous real world below. It is just the spot for polytechnic lecturer William Farmer to pursue his search for E. M. Forster and for his wife Fanny to get over a recent stillbirth. Just the setting, too, for some wicked observation of cultural pretensions and a host of kindly but wildly funny creations.

Janice Elliott manipulates her characters and her plot with a masterly and light touch. THE ITALIAN LESSON is a wry and clever novel about the British abroad, at once a modern reworking of Forster's themes and, at the same time, strikingly original.

'Janice Elliott is one of the best novelists writing in England'
Christopher Driver in The Guardian

'There is no doubt in my mind that she is one of the most resourceful and imaginative living English novelists'
Paul Bailey in The London Standard